COMING ATTRACTIONS
94

Edited by Douglas Glover & Maggie Helwig

This book was written and published with the assistance of the Canada Council, the Ontario Arts Council and others.

ISBN 0 88750 975 4 (hardcover)
ISBN 0 88750 976 2 (softcover)

Cover art by Ghitta Caiserman-Roth
Book design by Michael Macklem

Printed in Canada

PUBLISHED IN CANADA BY OBERON PRESS

Introduction

The great Russian Formalist Viktor Shklovsky once said that literature renders the world freshly visible by "making it strange." If there is one thing the writers included in this year's *Coming Attractions* share, it is a haunting strangeness of vision, an angle of perception at once acute, surprising and affecting. In part, this stems from the fact that two of the three are from Newfoundland, where the intersection of a vibrant oral tradition (and the rhythms of popular speech) with an imported literary modernism is creating a vigorous hybrid that is knowing and self-conscious while yet retaining a deep emotional impact. But all three are also individualists, obeying an authorial imperative to hew to a unique line and carve a phrase, a line, a story from the resisting mass of personal experience in a way no-one else has ever done.

Donald McNeill grew up in St. John's but left on a Rhodes Scholarship to Oxford and made himself a life in the high-profile world of television journalism, first at the CBC and later at CBS in the United States. His career climaxed in 1991 when he won an Emmy Award for reporting on the Soviet Union. Now he lives in York Harbour, Maine, crafting powerful, realistic and highly nuanced stories of an island world he clearly never left behind. McNeill's Newfoundland is redolent of past wars and past loves, a place where the melancholy beauty of the landscape is etched with a brooding sense of mortality: "A submariner's moon, the sailors called it, the light reflecting on the surface of the harbour and the sea outside in a cold merciless sheen that silhouetted their ships and made them easy prey for the U-boat wolfpacks....And streaming now through Jamie's window, it bathed his pale uplifted face and filled his bedroom with a ghostly blue aura."

Elise Levine lives in Toronto, and in sharp contrast to McNeill, writes of a shadow world, a world of self-mutilation, sado-masochistic sex and lesbian lovers, a world whose primary image is the kitsch horror-flick of the black-and-white era, when Boris Karloff and Bela Lugosi lurched their way across the silver screen, slightly comic images of an ingrown alienation. Levine's language is clipped, almost telegraphic, gritty and pregnant with sinister implication. Innocence and pastoral romance are turned on their heads. In "Angel," Levine's heroine recalls having her nipple pierced by her lover—"I sold some blow in the bars and bought a beat-up Chevy Nova for $500.00, and we'd drive it out of the city to where it was dry and dusty, the late August fields burning with goldenrod. We'd stop on dirt roads and my eyelids would sweat as I squinted against the two o'clock sun, and when you kissed me I remembered how it felt when you pushed the needle through me...."

Lisa Moore still lives in St. John's in a house with an upstairs window that overlooks the Narrows. She belongs to a group of Newfoundland writers called the Burning Rock which may one day rival the Montreal Storytellers or Fredericton's Ice-House Gang. Moore's stories are startling narratives shot through with machine-gun bursts of imagery that is as visual as you can get on the printed page. Art itself becomes a metaphor for the mystery of life in stories in which Moore's protagonists struggle for balance between children and lovers and the general strangeness of things. In "The Nipple of Paradise," an artist dips the narrator's husband's thumb in a can of gold pigment—"It looked like a fragment of an ancient statue was somehow attached to his living hand....It made me think that love is made of isolated flashes and they are what we crave. It was getting dark outside Volker's studio and Cy's thumb glowed like something expensive, timeless."

DOUGLAS GLOVER

6

D. F. MCNEILL

Cosy and Nell

"Ignatius Loyola Fleming! In the name of God, stop this thing! Oh my God!"

The BSA motorbike was hurtling down a dirt road, yawing wildly from side to side in the loose gravel, even with the sidecar or perhaps because of it. The bike's driver, Loy Fleming, his teeth bared to the wind beneath his leather aviator's helmet and goggles, clutched the bucking handlebars and corrected the skids with abrupt, sickening jolts. He glanced from time to time at the sidecar where Nell Cluett, her bobbed hair bouncing, hung on with both hands while screaming at him. And Loy would grin at her and bellow again:

"The Lone Eagle is landing, Nell!... The Lone Eagle is landing!"

Seated on the pillion, pressing it tightly between his soccer-player's thighs, "Cosy" Lyall had his arms wrapped around Loy's waist Cosy's head was down, his face pressing against the back of his buddy's shoulder, the stiff leather of Loy's jacket smooth and cool on his cheek. He was facing out toward Nell, his fiancée of two years, grinning helplessly at her. Because of the racket—the roar of the bike's engine, the rattling tattoo of the stones on the mudguards—he could hear only snatches of Loy's teasing cry whipping by on the wind. But for once Cosy wasn't really concerned about Nell's needs: the Eagle was coming back and *he* was going to meet him at last.

It was the afternoon of 12 July, 1933, and Colonel Charles Lindbergh was about to land his Lockheed float plane on Bay Bulls Big Pond in Newfoundland. In the six years since Lindbergh's historic trans-Atlantic solo flight, Cosy Lyall had read the Colonel's version of his passage over St. John's so many times he had memorized it:

I came upon it suddenly—the little city of St. John's, after skimming over the top of a creviced granite summit—flat-roofed houses and stores, nestled at the edge of a deep harbour. It's almost completely surrounded by mountains. Farther ahead, the entrance to the harbour is a narrow gap with sides running up steeply to the crest of a low coastal range that holds back to the ocean. Fishing boats are riding at buoys and moored at wharves.

Twilight deepens as I plunge into the valley. Mountains behind screen off the colours of the western sky. For me, this northern city is the last point on the last island of America—the end of land: the end of day.

And here Cosy's heart always quickened:

There's no time to circle, no fuel to waste. It takes only a moment, stick forward, engine throttled. To dive down over the wharves (men stop the after-supper chores to look upward), over the ships in the harbour (a rowboat's oars lose their rhythm as I pass), and out through the gap, that doorway to the Atlantic. Mountain sides slip by on either wing. Great rollers break in spray against their base. The hulk of a wrecked ship lies high upon the boulders. North America and its islands are behind. Ireland is two thousand miles ahead.

"See that part in brackets, see that there," Cosy would way many times after Lindbergh's triumph, stabbing his finger at his dog-eared magazine and reading aloud, "'a rowboat's oars lose their rhythm as I pass.'"

And then he would look up, triumphant too, at whomever he had buttonholed. "Well that was me, buddy! That was me out rowing in that boat! The Colonel left out about waggling his wings at me when he went over, but that's what he did, I swear to it."

That wasn't exactly true. Cosy had been carrying a message out to the captain of one of his firm's schooners moored in the harbour; he was being rowed by a crewman and he couldn't remember if the man had stopped rowing or not when the Spirit of St. Louis had roared overhead. As for the waggling wings, it had all happened so fast he wasn't really sure. But there had been some kind of movement, of that he was certain.

Regardless of detail, on that fateful day it was as if Lindbergh had reached down and plucked Duncan Lyall up out of the harbour and lifted him to new heights, to a lofty place from which he would look at the world differently in his imagination forever after. Cosy had never thought of Signal Hill as a "mountain" or the South Side Hills as "a coastal range." And where was the "creviced granite summit" that the Eagle had skimmed when coming in over the harbour? Mount Pearl? Kenmount? Nagle's Hill? Those were granite summits? He had never thought of those places in such an exotic way, had never viewed his island as he might a foreign land.

Before Lindbergh, Cosy's imagination had been mired in the Great War—which he had greatly regretted missing out on. Now, his horizons expanded, he had for the first time in his life a new sense—a highly romantic sense, it was true—of his own island as being just one among the many foreign places on the planet. And he wanted to soar someday, like Lindbergh, "out through the gap" (known to Cosy as The Narrows) and beyond the confines of the steep-sided, womb-like harbour from which he had first seen the Lone Eagle.

Loy turned his head and yelled, "We're going to be the first to meet him. An exclusive!"

Thirty minutes earlier there had been five hundred cars and two thousand people assembled along the narrow road that ran past the pebbled shore of Bay Bulls Big Pond. Like Cosy and Nell and Loy, most of the people had been there since midday, boiling tea kettles and making a picnic of the event.

When they first arrived, Loy, a reporter for the *Daily Telegram* assigned to cover the story, was able to talk to two men wearing blazers and white duck pants down at the dock where a motor-launch was tied up. Loy had the big-boned build of a brawler and rugged good looks. He had removed his leather biking jacket and held it slung casually over his shoulder as he talked. He wore an open-necked shirt, no tie, and his curly reddish hair was an unruly mess after pulling off his helmet. He seemed relaxed as he asked questions, but when he returned to Cosy and Nell the humorous gleam was gone from his blue eyes.

"It's going to be like bloody royalty," he snapped. He jerked his head at the dock. "If those flunkies have their way we won't get anywhere near the Lindberghs." He paused. "'The Strawbridges are coming to *receive* them,'" he said, aping an English accent. "That's what they just said. And you can bet they'll toss them in that bloody great Daimler of theirs and whisk them away downtown as fast as they can. I'll be lucky to get a quote."

They had chosen a spot among some low shrubs. Nell sat with her legs tucked under her wide skirt, smoothing down the blanket they had spread out for their picnic. She wore a white shirt with a narrow blue tie, a white wool cardigan draped over her shoulders. Cosy also wore a tie, a freshly ironed shirt and plus fours. He bought his clothes at a small discount in one of the departments of the Water Street firm where he worked as a floorwalker. He had removed his belted jacket, carefully folding it, and was now crouched near the blanket, piling together the sticks and twigs he had gathered for a fire to boil water.

"That's Jimmy Warren from Harvey's down on the dock, isn't it?" Nell said.

"Bloody *bourgeois* snob! That's who he is," Loy said. "It's always the same with those capitalist sleeveens on Water Street." Again he mimicked an English accent. "'If you're going to be called *gentlemen* of the press then you should *dress* like gentlemen.' That's what that squabby little bastard said to me. Excuse my language, but I'd break his goddam neck if I could find it."

Cosy, still hunkered, laughed and crooned, "If you're Irish, stay out of my parrr-lourrr..."

"He's always so stuck up, Jimmy Warren is," Nell said. "Here, comb your hair." And she passed Loy a comb from her handbag.

Cosy chanted, "'Like all dirty St. John's streels/He dressed his head before his heels.'"

Loy made as if to kick him and Cosy hopped back and up to his feet with agility, snorting air through his nostrils and throwing his fists as if he were shadow boxing. "Now Dempsey's got that Irish fake, Fleming, on the ropes...one two one two...the *Manassa Mauler* is merciless..."

"Oh Duncan! Grow up and stop that!" Nell said sharply— she refused to call him Cosy. She turned to Loy. "Who's the other one? I've never seen him before. He looks foreign."

"Arthur Winslow," Loy said. "He's American, down here for Pan American who're paying for all this. It's nothing but big business."

Eagerly, Cosy explained to Nell again how Pan American was setting up to go trans-Atlantic; that the company was using the Lindberghs, the Colonel and his wife Anne, to scout out landing spots for their big flying boats; that Harvey's was Pan Am's agent in St. John's.

"Lindbergh's getting paid for it," Loy said when Cosy finished. "He's not doing anybody any favours."

"Yeah, maybe, but you can't keep him out of the sky," Cosy said. "Look at all the miles he's done on this. He just loves to fly."

Nell was staring at the lake, as if distracted by some thought. She was a full-bodied young woman, a year older than Cosy, a year younger than Loy. Her short hair was a glossy black and she had a round face with large dark eyes; her smile was crooked and attractive. Sometimes when she spoke, her mouth pulled down at one corner, giving a sarcastic shading to her speech. But not this time:

"She lost her baby," she said softly. "Maybe they just want

to get away from all the publicity about the kidnapping. Be alone together..."

As her voice trailed off she looked at Loy, who had been watching her. Loy quickly turned to Cosy.

"Cosy, my boy, you've got to stop being so naïve," he said. "I've told you before and I'll tell you again. Lindbergh got paid $250,000 for that article you've been carrying around for donkey's years. That's ten times the prize money for the solo flight itself, and you're trying to tell me it's all for the love of flying?" He raised his arm dramatically and pointed a finger at the sky. "It's dangerous up there. Remember that crazy German, Urban Diteman? Up at Lester's Field a few years ago? Where is he now? Down in the drink and dead, that's where! You don't do that kind of thing unless there's publicity, my boy. It's all promotion and big bucks."

Cosy grinned. He knew Loy had ambitions, someday, to be a bigtime journalist and writer like his idol, Hemingway. "You're just a phony cynic," he teased. "You're jealous because they hardly pay you a living wage for that stuff you write in the *Daily Telegram* and the Eagle gets two hundred and..."

Loy lunged at him, roaring, "You ungrateful little runt. I made your name in this town."

Cosy was slender, the smaller of the two, but faster. He dodged back quickly and stuck up his fists, his curled fingers toward his face like in the pictures he had seen of John L. Sullivan. The two friends sparred for a moment, then grappled and fell to the ground, laughing and pummelling each other on the upper arms as they rolled about. Loy soon pinned Cosy on his back, straddling him and pulling up on his necktie.

"They could hang you like this and you'd still be dreaming," he said.

While they ate and drank tea, the two men argued about airplanes and engines: whether Urban Diteman in his *Golden Hind*, the Barling monoplane in which the German daredevil had dazzled them with aerobatics before he had disappeared over the cold Atlantic, had fatally stressed aerodynamics over horsepower.

"The Spirit of St. Louis was a flying gas tank," Loy said. "Lindbergh couldn't even see out the front. Diteman could have flown rings around him."

"Yeah, but the Spirit was a high-wing monoplane. The Lockheed he's bringing in here is something different. You just watch the Eagle fly this time. And don't forget horse-power, Loy. This plane's got seven hundred horses. All you want is show. But you can't sacrifice power for performance. The Strawbridge's Daimler's got more horsepower than that little kite Diteman flew. You always forget about horse-power..."

"Loy forgot his tool kit, too," Nell interrupted. She was lying back on one elbow, watching them, playing with a straw at her mouth in a way that made her bottom lip pout. "You can't fix an engine without a tool kit. What happened to it, Loy?"

Cosy looked at her, puzzled by her *non sequitur*. Then he rolled over on the blanket and looked at the bike nearby. "She's right. It's gone." He sat up and looked at Loy. "Think we lost it on the way out here?"

Loy shook his head. "No. I lost it a few days ago."

Cosy turned to Nell. "You got sharp eyes, honeybunch. When did you notice?"

"In the newspaper," Nell said, looking at Loy. "Lost and found. Somewhere between Circular Road and on your way home to Kilbride wasn't it?"

Loy looked down at the blanket, the tips of his ears turning pink.

Nell said, "Now who do we know that lives on Circular Road, I wonder?"

"Are you a detective?" Cosy said. "Hot damn! I'm engaged to a female Dash Hammett."

"Oh shut up, Duncan!" Nell said in a play-acting voice, tempering her words with a saucy smile. She pointed down

14

the beach to where some men were kicking a soccer ball about. "Why don't you go play football while I find out who Loy's newest *belle* is."

Cosy obeyed, grinning at Loy as he hopped to his feet. "You're in trouble now," he said. "Once she gets her hooks into you, you don't have a chance."

The men with the soccer ball stopped playing as Cosy trotted up to them. A few of them clapped their hands.

"It's Cosy!...Cosy Lyall!"

"Hey, Cosy! How's it going?"

One of the men tossed the ball to Cosy. He caught it deftly on his instep, balanced it there for a moment before flipping it in the air. He bounced it back in the air again with his head, next with his knee, and again with his instep. Then, over and over—foot, head, knee—he kept the ball going until, finally, he flicked it over his head, caught it with the back of his heel, and expertly shot it across to the hands of the man who had tossed it to him.

"Mind if I join in a little game, fellas?" he said with a shy smile.

The men were grinning with delight. Sure, they said. Great. Then one of them said, "You trust that other fella with your girl, Cosy? Better watch him. He's moving in."

Cosy looked back and saw that Loy had shifted on the blanket closer to Nell. He was leaning toward her talking. Cosy smiled at the joke. Loy was his best friend, had been since the time when he started to rise as a football player.

Now, Cosy was a St. John's All-Star who played outside right for the Guards in the city's Senior League. Sailors from the Royal Navy fleet that called at the port and who played against the All-Stars said that he was good enough to play professional in England. His nickname had come from Loy's pen a few years earlier—"Lyall has made the corner kick a form of art," Loy wrote. "Left footed or right, he can curl the ball toward the goal and *cosy* it in past the post by inches for a score."

Loy, who was not a sports writer—he didn't care much for team efforts—had been assigned to do a profile piece on the rising young football star. He went to the locker-room after the game and found himself looking into a boyish, guileless face with shy hazel eyes. Twenty-four-year old Duncan Lyall was bashful, self-effacing—he treated Loy like *he* was the star. They spent a few days together, Loy ferreting out Cosy's story.

As is often the case, Loy learned a lot more than he wrote. Cosy's father had died drunk in an accident when Cosy was very young subsequently, he had had to drop out of school in Grade 8 in order to work and support his mother. His three older brothers had gone off to the Great War where one had been killed and one so badly wounded he was an invalid and unemployable. A third brother had survived without a scratch, but had gone to Detroit to find work in the fledgling automobile industry. The Masonic Lodge had looked after the family ever since the father's death, and when young Duncan was old enough to work it was the Masons who had found him a job with one of the big merchant firms on Water Street. He had joined as a messenger boy at thirteen and had worked his way up to floorwalker.

Cosy and Nell were already engaged when Loy came on the scene. Nell was a secretary at the courthouse, an outport girl who lived in a hostel for young working women. Her past was somewhat mysterious. She had travelled for some years to Canada and the Boston states with her father, Captain Cluett, working as his secretary in the fish-selling business. She hinted to Cosy that she had been engaged before, but had changed her mind when she judged the man to be unreliable. That was her favourite quality in a man, she said—reliability. Nell liked the new flapper fashions, and pressed Cosy to take her out to the old pavilions turned roadhouses—Donovans, Woodstock, Smithville—and to the new nightclubs built closer to the city after the war—The Old Colony, Bellavista. She like the wild new dances, the Blackbottom and the Lindy, but she wouldn't smoke cigarettes or drink much, perhaps out of deference to Cosy who didn't smoke because he was an athlete and didn't drink because alcohol terrified him. Cosy couldn't afford a car, but he was a popular sports figure and they easily found rides to the roadhouses and clubs with other couples. At first Nell enjoyed Cosy's popularity and the attention that surrounded them. But later she used it to precipitate their engagement, claiming that Cosy was humiliating her with his indifference as to how others saw *her* position. Cosy hastened to please her with a formal engagement, but because he had his mother to look after the day was not yet forseeable when they could afford to get married.

Nell was Cosy's first serious romance—he was shy and had always been too busy working or playing football—and he was inexperienced with women. Nell allowed necking and some very light petting, but even after they became engaged there was no sex. Cosy confessed to Loy that he remained a virgin.

Now, playing on the beach, Cosy was aiming to head the ball when he saw the floatplane. It was about five miles west of the lake in a cloudless sky. He stepped aside, letting the ball fall to the ground, keeping his eyes on the plane.

Lindbergh!

Others saw or heard the plane, too. People were calling out and pointing. He turned and looked over to Nell and Loy. They were paying no attention. It was Nell doing the talking now, very earnestly it seemed, and Loy had his head down, listening. Cosy started running toward them.

"Lindbergh!" he yelled. "It's Lindbergh! The Lone Eagle is landing!"

Loy looked up at Cosy, then to the sky. He got up quickly. Nell stayed on the blanket.

"He's starting to circle for an approach," Cosy said excitedly. He punched Loy on the arm. "The Lone Eagle is landing!"

"I'm not so sure," Loy said. "He's pretty far away."

The low-winged floatplane completed its circle without coming anywhere near the lake. It straightened course and headed away north, toward the city.

"Jesus Christ!" Loy said. "He's lost and heading for St. John's. He'll see the floatplanes down at Quidi Vidi and land there. Come on!"

There was a great rush to the cars all along the beach, people cramming into them. Then the cars were backing up, bumping, honking, jerking forward, backfiring. The traffic quickly snarled and dozens of men stood waving their arms and shouting directions that went unheard in the cacophony of horns and racing engines. Occasionally, like a cod spurting from a trap, single cars broke loose and fishtailed down the road to St. John's in a swirl of dust.

Loy and Cosy and Nell, well ahead of the others on the motorbike, had almost reached Kilbride on the outskirts of the city when Nell pointed to the sky. It was Lindbergh's plane, coming back.

Loy stopped the bike and lifted his goggles. All three of them craned their necks as the Lockheed floatplane droned overhead. This time it was heading straight for Bay Bulls Big Pond.

"Make up your bloody mind!" Loy shouted up at the aircraft.

"Come on, let's go!" Cosy cried. "We've got to get back."

Loy turned the bike around and revved the engine. He pulled down his goggles and looked over his shoulder at Cosy.

"The Lone Eagle is landing!" he shouted, grinning. He glanced out at Nell in the sidecar. "Hang on now, Nell!"

They had the Lindberghs all to themselves for a good ten minutes. The Colonel, tall and gangly, stood on the front of one of the Lockheed's floats, less than 50 feet from the rickety dock. He laughed and apologized when Loy told him about the confusion he had caused—he had landed at Quidi Vidi where he'd been given directions to Big Pond. He anwered

Loy's questions in a good-natured way, then asked for news about the progress of Air Marshal Italo Balbo.

The commercial air race was on to capture the new trans-Atlantic market, and the Italians, possible competitors with Pan American, were also prospecting for suitable routes. Air Marshal Balbo and his armada of 24 Savia-Marchetti flying boats had left Italy on 5 July with the blessings of Mussolini, en route to Chicago via Iceland and Labrador. They had reached Iceland several days ago.

"He left Iceland for Cartwright early this morning," Loy said. "I hope the *fascist* bastard freezes to death."

Lindbergh stiffened but said nothing. He looked unhappy with the comment.

Nell, standing back with Cosy, whispered that Lindbergh was so good looking. His light brown hair was tousled and he had a cute little cleft in his chin. "Look at his eyes," she whispered, "they're so sensitive and sad. It must be because of the baby." Lindbergh's wife waved to them, but stayed in her open cockpit.

Cosy was tongue-tied until Loy, finished with his questions, elbowed him. Then he blurted across the gap of water:

"Do you remember when you flew over the harbour, Colonel? There was a rowboat and the fella stopped rowing?"

Lindbergh looked puzzled, then nodded slowly. "Yeah, I think so."

Cosy nodded too, grinning happily now. "Yeah," he echoed, tapping his chest. "That was me, Colonel. That was me in that boat. And you waggled your wings at me when you went over. Do you remember that?"

Lindbergh stared at him for a moment, then he grinned too. "Yeah, sure. I remember that. Nice to meet you at last."

"Lyall's the name. Duncan Lyall. They call me Cosy around here. I sure wish I could shake your hand."

"Sure," Lindbergh said. "Soon as I get off this kite."

He looked over their heads to the road. "Looks like the reception committee is arriving now."

Within minutes, the dock and the area around it were crowded. Then Harvey's man, Jimmy Warren, was there, shouting:

"Off this dock immediately! Clear off!"

"Bugger you!" Loy said. But he had his quotes and he pushed his way out through the crowd.

Cosy stayed, hoping for his handshake. The motorlaunch went out to the aircraft and directed Lindbergh to the mooring buoy for the Lockheed. Once ashore, Lindbergh's wife was presented with a bouquet of flowers by Mrs. Strawbridge, then the couple were hustled over to the Daimler as Loy had predicted. The crowd pressed in, cheering, and Cosy, his hand outstretched, almost made it to the car window before the Daimler pulled away.

Disappointed, Cosy kicked at the pebbles. It was a moment before he remembered Nell. He had forgotten all about her in his excitement and in the crush. He stood on his toes and looked around. Finally, he saw her and Loy, off by themselves along the shore. They looked like they were arguing.

Then Nell reached up and slapped Loy's face, hard.

The following day, Cosy saw Loy's byline beneath the front page banner in the *Daily Telegram*—LINDBERGH LANDS TWICE ON ARRIVAL—but not Loy himself. The two of them had planned to go back to Big Pond that day for Lindbergh's departure but Cosy had to cancel.

Nell wouldn't let him.

She had stormed off without explanation at Big Pond, catching a ride back to the city in one of the cars. Cosy, left alone on the shore with Loy, had asked what had happened.

"Ah, it was nothing," Loy said. "She'll get over it."

"But why did she slap you?"

"Well, she just kept on prying about who I was seeing down on Circular Road. You know how women are about things like that. They're nosy, that's what. Anyway, I finally got fed up and told her to mind her own business. Maybe I used stronger language than that, but anyway, she just hauls off and slaps me one across the chops."

Cosy was shaking his head.

"Maybe I said she was having her rags on," Loy added. "Or something like that. I'm sorry."

"Hot damn!" Cosy said, his strongest expletive. He knew what "having her rags on" meant, but not much else about women's menstrual cycles. "Why'd you say that? She's really proper about things like that."

Later that evening, Cosy went to Nell's hostel to try to patch things up. She was still smouldering and her dark eyes blazed when Cosy told her partly what Loy had said, the part about her prying. "There's more to it than that," she said mysteriously. Loy was a womanizer, she went on, a bad influence. And between football and racing around with Loy, Cosy hardly had any time for her.

"You're just not reliable when you're with him, Duncan. You're going to have to chose between him and me or you can have your ring back right now."

Cosy telephoned Loy early the next morning. Before he could say a word Loy was ranting about the editorial in his own paper: it wasn't about Lindbergh at all, but instead praised Balbo's Italian air squadron for successfully crossing the North Atlantic from Iceland to Cartwright in Labrador. Cosy waited him out, then told him that he had to bow out of going to Big Pond to see Lindbergh's departure. He told him that Nell was jealous of the time they spent together, but that he thought she would cool down in a few weeks. Meanwhile, he was going to have to spend more time with her to keep her happy. He didn't mention Nell's ultimatum.

There was a long pause at the other end before Loy said, "I understand. Cheer up now and I'll see you soon."

Cosy missed being with Loy. Loy was a great talker, he thought, and funny too. Loy had two years of college at Memorial and he spouted grand theories about history and what was happening in the world, including a lot of talk about

Russia and the revolution that was coming elsewhere. "Only two ways to go, Cosy. Join the Revolution or look out for Number One. Now there's only one choice in that for a decent caring man, isn't there?"

Cosy, Loy said, was being exploited by the merchant capitalists on Water Street, just like the fishermen. He tried to explain the class system simply: half the island was on the dole, he said, but among the crowd out at Murray's Pond Country Club and Baly Haly Golf Club you'd never know there was a depression. Cosy thought that that was the natural order of things and considered himself lucky to have a job. He didn't understand any of it, but he enjoyed ribbing Loy. When he became well-off, he said, he'd also belong to Murray's Pond or Baly Haly. Or both. Besides, he said, he didn't fancy being compared to a fisherman.

Loy was also a sympathetic listener, even when Cosy talked about how much he minded missing out on the Great War, a war that Loy said had been waged for the benefit of the capitalists and that they had been lucky to avoid. The most sacred day on the island was 1 July, the day the Blue Puttees of the Royal Newfoundland Regiment had been decimated at Beaumont Hamel in 1916. On the anniversary of that day, Cosy said, you felt all around you as if you could never become a man because you weren't in that war. Cosy never missed the big parade and the service at the War Memorial, laying a wreath for his dead brother and fighting to hold back his tears when the band played "Oh God Our Help In Ages Past."

Loy also listened when Cosy talked about his dreams of travel, about sailing out the Narrows and seeing the world, about what it would be like to do great things like Lindbergh. He couldn't talk to Nell about any of that. But one night, not long after missing Lindbergh's departure, Cosy discovered a compensation. He and Nell were at the Lyall house where Cosy lived with his mother, a very modest home in a poorer part of the city called Rabbit Town. The old woman had gone up to bed, the couple were entwined on a sofa, listening to soft music on the radio, necking. Nell became more passionate than usual. Cosy was erect.

"Oh Cosy," Nell murmured, "I can't stand it waiting anymore. Love me."

Cosy was clumsy but, with Nell's help, he was successful. Astonished with the pleasure he felt, he became an ardent lover. "You're going to get me pregnant," Nell warned, yet succumbing to his ardour. Then, at the end of July, she said she thought she might be pregnant; that they might have to get married sooner than they had planned.

On the evening of 1 August, Cosy and the All-Stars played an exhibition match against an Italian navy team selected from the crews of the two submarines and the supply ship, *Biglieri*, which were anchored in St. John's harbour. The fog was so thick the Italian goalkeeper never saw the ball on one of Cosy's corner kicks until it was sailing past him into the upper corner of the goal for the only score of the match. Afterwards, amidst the noisy celebration in the locker-room, a reporter for the *Daily Telegram* found Cosy and gave him a note.

It was from Loy who was out at Trinity Bay on a story. Air Marshal Italo Balbo and his fleet of flying boats had landed at Shoal Harbour on their return flight from Chicago to Italy; the same foul weather that had helped Cosy score on a corner kick had delayed the Italian's departure for Valencia. The note said the Air Marshal and his entourage were coming to St. John's by train the following day to meet with the officers and crews of the Italian ships in the harbour. Later, there would be a dance for the airmen and sailors—officers only—at the Newfoundland Hotel. Loy had included two tickets in the envelope with his note.

Nell couldn't resist the opportunity to hobnob with the fast set, Loy or no Loy. She read the advertisements—*Chic Summer Hats: Every lady who delights in smart headwear will be charmed with the new shipment (just opened) of The New White Mesh Hats (in fashionable shapes)*—and bought a new hat. When she and

Cosy arrived at the hotel they found their table to be one of a few reserved for the press at the back of the ballroom. Nell ordered a Gibson, Cosy a ginger ale. Loy wasn't there yet.

One of the newsmen told Cosy that Air Marshal Balbo was having dinner on the *Biglieri* and Loy was down at the harbour hoping to catch him. "I'll tell you, Cosy, Loy's gone real venomy on this Italian thing. Two weeks or more now he's been raving. Ever since that editorial in the Telegram calling Balbo and his crowd 'our Italian friends.' Sousing a lot on the rum too."

The news worried Cosy, the drinking part especially. He hoped Loy wasn't going to get himself in trouble. Also, he felt guilty. Loy needed somebody to blow off steam with and as Loy's best friend he had always been that somebody. He had let his buddy down. And would Loy bother to listen to him now? He had been hoping to blow off some steam himself. He wanted to tell Loy about Nell and him, about how he had made her pregnant and their having to get married sooner, even though they couldn't afford to. On the one hand, he felt boastful about it, something that even scoring goals had never made him feel. One the other hand, he was terrified.

Cosy kept an eye on the wide doorway while he and Nell danced a foxtrot. The ballroom was decorated with streamers in the Italian national colours—red, white, and green—and with Union Jack bunting on the bandstand. The space was filling up, a number of the local men wearing the dress uniforms of the Royal Newfoundland Regiment. The same Strawbridge who had been Lindbergh's host wore the insignia of Lieutenant Colonel of the Regiment, although Cosy knew that he had never been overseas during the Great War. The women wore ballgowns and jewellery.

Abruptly, Nell stopped dancing and went back to the table. She quickly took off her new hat and gulped at her Gibson. "I'm embarrassed," she whispered angrily to Cosy. "I'm the only one out there with a stupid hat on. All these women are done up for a fancy dress ball. I thought you said it was a summer dance."

"I did," Cosy said. "I mean I thought it was. It was supposed to be." He looked pained, as if the women's dresses and jewellery were his fault. "But listen, you look wonderful, and they're just putting on airs for the Italians..."

He was interrupted by applause, scattered at first, but quickly thickening. It swelled to a rhythmic smacking of palms. The band straggled to a halt. There was a commotion at the entrance nearby. Then Cosy saw Italian officers in shiny jackboots spilling into the room around the edges of the doorway. They wore dazzling white uniforms dripping with braid, black shirts and black ties. In the middle of the doorway, a noisy knot of men was slowly moving forward. A few flashbulbs popped. Some of the men were walking backwards. Loy was one of them.

"Why don't you answer me?" Loy shouted. "Are you looking for military bases?"

At the centre of the knot, Air Marshal Balbo ignored Loy's question and smiled broadly all around. He was square-jawed and barrel-chested. He wore a black peakless cap with an eagle insignia, like the one Cosy had seen Mussolini wearing in the Pathé newsreels. He had his thumb tucked under the leather shoulder strap of his Sam Browne, his hand resting inches above his holstered pistol.

"I think it is truly a beautiful city," he said loudly in English. "A distinct Nordic stamp about it."

Loy again. "Why do you have so many aircraft?"

Balbo. "And you islanders! Your Prime Minister and the other representatives of the Government are so splendid. Yet the people are so charmingly naïve and natural."

The knot dissolved at the edge of the dance floor, Loy and the photographers brushed aside by the local notables. Lieutenant Colonel Strawbridge drew himself up stiffly and saluted. Balbo responded with a flip of his forearm up from the elbow in the Italian fascist salute. The band struck up a lively tango.

"Hey Loy!" Cosy called, pulling on his friend's arm, turning him.

Loy stared at him, hostility lingering in his eyes. Cosy had never seen him so dishevelled, a reddish stubble on his face, his eyes bloodshot, his hair a tangled mop. His clothes were rumpled and he wore no tie. He smelled of booze. Cosy felt panic, as if he were losing control instead of Loy. He had never seen Loy like this before. Not on any story, or anywhere. Ever. What was going on? The way Loy was behaving wasn't him. It wasn't right.

"It's me! Cosy! Are you all right?"

For the briefest moment Loy looked annoyed. "For Christ's sake! I know who you are," he said. He glanced over his shoulder and back. "Did you see that? Did you see that fucking salute?"

"Yeah, yeah, I saw it. It's kind of funny. Like it's not a real salute..."

Loy suddenly grinned and gripped Cosy's shoulder. "Good to see you," he said loudly. "Glad you could make it." He looked around the room. "Did Nell come too?"

"Sure she did. And listen, buddy! Have I got something to tell you." Cosy looked about. It was too public. He took Loy's arm. "Come on over and say hello to Nell first."

"Nah, not yet," Loy said quickly. "I got to get cleaned up a bit. I've been up since yesterday and then that train ride from Clarenville. But first I need a drink."

He pulled his arm free and peeled away toward the bar. Cosy hesitated, looked over to his table for Nell. The lights had been dimmed and he couldn't see her through the crowd. He followed Loy to the bar.

People had already cleared a space around Loy. They were giving him what Cosy called snooty looks. Loy got a double rum and Coke.

"That man doesn't belong here. Somebody should evict him."

The speaker, a middle-aged woman with a pinched face and tightly permed hair like a helmet, was glaring at Loy. She wore a black sheath dress and a pearl choker.

Loy turned, resting one elbow on the bar, and raised his glass to her. "Nice necklace. Bet that could feed a few of the starving babes over on Lime Street or Carter's Hill." He leered at the woman. "You wouldn't be a slum landlord now by any chance, would you? The way you talk about eviction, you know, I just wondered if you were, and how many of the suffering poor you're going to put out in the cold this winter…"

Cosy stepped in front of Loy and turned him away from the woman. "Come on, Loy," he urged, keeping his voice low. "You'll get in trouble."

"Sure, I got to have a piss anyway," Loy said loudly. And as Cosy towed him off he looked back at the woman and drew a finger across his throat. "Comes the revolution…swishhhh!"

They were alone in the men's room.

"Listen, I got to tell you this," Cosy said excitedly. He glanced again at the door—he'd already checked for feet inside the stalls. Loy stood pissing, his body slightly inclined, both hands resting on the shoulder-height rim of one of the giant marble urinals that stood along the wall like up-ended sarcophagi.

"Nell is sure she's pregnant and we got to get married right away. And I don't care what she says, you're going to be my best man."

Loy's body stiffened a little. He turned his head slowly to look at Cosy. He was silent.

"Well?" Cosy said, grinning proudly. "Aren't you going to say anything?" He did a little dance, clicking his heels on the tiles. "I did it, Loy! I finally did it! And it was wonderful! A virgin no more! And I love it!"

Loy shook himself, buttoned up and turned to face Cosy.

"And when did this wondrous deflowering happen?"

Cosy waggled his head, still grinning. "I don't know. About two weeks ago. What does it matter?"

Loy snorted. "It matters because it takes more than that, you twillick."

"But I've done it more than once. Lots of times now."

"Jesus H. Christ! No! You don't get it!" Loy looked fierce. "It's not the number of times you do it that counts, Cosy. It takes more *time* than two weeks for her to know if she's pregnant. A couple of months at least. You get it now? If she *is* pregnant, then it can't be yours."

Cosy's expression had changed from puzzled to hurt; his mouth opened and closed and opened again but no sound came out. Loy lurched a couple of steps, gripped him by the shoulders and shook him. Cosy could smell the rum.

"Listen!" Loy said. "You don't *have* to marry her. She..."

"You mean she's lying about it?"

Loy stopped shaking, but held on, staring into Cosy's face.

"No, I didn't say that. But it can't be yours. She's just a bay wop trying to trap you. Can't you see?" He shook Cosy again. "Anyway, where's it written a man's got to get married if a woman gets pregnant? Tell me, where? That's old-fashioned duckedy-mud shit, Cosy. Bourgeois bilge! They don't know what's happening away from this frigging island. There's a new world being born out there, that's what. There's free love, and if you don't want to have kids then there's proper abortions with doctors. They already got it in Russia, Cosy. And when socialism comes you won't have those starving babes down on Lime Street like I told that rich bitch out there. Jesus fucking Christ! Who'd want to bring a child into what we got here anyway!"

Loy drew in a deep breath, held it, then exhaled noisily through his lips. He let his arms fall from Cosy's shoulders. Cosy couldn't stand the smell of Loy's breath and he turned his head, closing his eyes.

28

"Don't call her that," he said, still turned away.

"What? A rich bitch?"

Cosy looked at Loy, his bottom lip trembling now. "No. I mean Nell. Don't call her a bay wop. And your breath is fausty."

The door opened and two men came in on the blast of music and human voices. One of them, a member of the extended family that owned the merchant company where Cosy worked, looked surprised. "Well, Cosy," he said, "you're stepping up in the world I see." He looked at Loy on his way to the urinals and frowned—word had spread about the scene at the bar. "The Italians say you played a superb game last night, Cosy," he called over his shoulder. "Congratulations. But you musn't let the firm's side down you know. Must watch the company you keep."

Loy was swinging his head melodramatically back and forth between the urinals and Cosy's face, as if anticipating a reaction. Cosy remained silent.

"You going to take that?" Loy shouted. "That fascist shimmick is threatening you! You don't have to take that! Come on!" He grabbed Cosy's arm and pulled him to the door, singing loudly as he went: "Arise ye prisoners of starvation!...Arise ye wretched of the earth..."

When they stepped into the din of the ballroom, Loy's singing was swallowed up. "That'll show 'em," Loy bellowed. "C'mon, I'll buy you a drink."

Cosy pulled his arm free. He didn't care now what trouble Loy got into that night. He had to get to Nell. There had to be an explanation.

"I don't drink, Loy," he shouted. "I don't drink! Remember!"

He left Loy and started skirting the perimeter of the ballroom. It was dim and thick with smoke, including the pungent smell of foreign cigarettes. The band was thumping out nothing but tangos; the dance floor, sprinkled with the white uniformed Italians, looked like the cloth in a salt-and-pepper cap. The foreigners were executing fantastic glissades that brought whoops of delight from the local ladies.

Nell was alone at the table and in a fury. She had a Gibson, half full, and the waiter hadn't taken away her empties. Cosy counted four, which was unusual for her.

"Where *have* you been?" she demanded. "I've been sitting here like a wallflower for hours. You've been with Loy Fleming, haven't you? And you promised not to..."

She stopped and looked up at Cosy's face looming over her. Something she saw in it made her anger wilt instantly, and instead she looked like she was going to cry.

Cosy pulled a chair up close and sat down. "It doesn't matter where I've been, Nell, I just want to know the truth." His bottom lip was trembling again. "Are you really pregnant? Because if you are Loy says it can't be mine because it's too soon. And if you're not then why are you lying to me?"

Nell turned pale as he spoke and put her hands to her face. Behind her hands there came now a muffled sobbing. Cosy could hear only snatches of what she was saying. "Loy, Loy, Loy—all you ever care about—his fault—beginning."

"What do you mean? All his fault. How?"

Nell's hands came down below her eyes. "It's Loy's baby. He did it to me and he won't take me..." She sobbed again and her hands went back up.

"He won't what? What won't he do?"

Cosy pulled at her forearm and Nell opened her hands. Then, suddenly, she reached out and clutched at Cosy, her eyes wide, her mascara smeared on her wet cheeks.

"You've got to marry me, Cosy," she cried hoarsely. "You've got to! Please! I didn't mean to hurt you."

The band stopped suddenly and Nell's last words carried beyond the table. But nobody turned to look. Instead, people were getting up and craning their necks to see up front where a struggle was going on. Then a bunched-up group of men came quickly up the middle of the dance floor, roughly push-

ing and pulling Loy, half-carrying him toward the doorway.
Loy was shouting and trying to punch at the men who were
throwing him out.

Cosy stood up as Loy went past, Nell hanging on to his arm.
But he didn't try to follow.

A few days later, Cosy learned that Loy had been fired because
of the ruckus at the dance. It had started when Loy called Air
Marshal Balbo a fascist swine in front of Lieutenant-Colonel
Strawbridge and then tried to punch him. But what really did
him in was taking a shot at Strawbridge himself when that
epitome of the establishment tried to intervene, and calling
the Colonel a chinless coward who was unworthy to lead the
valorous Blue Puttees of the Royal Newfoundland Regiment.
One phone call to the publishers of the *Daily Telegram* the
next day finished for good Loy's journalism career on the
island.

It was Nell who told Cosy that Loy had been planning to
leave anyway, so he wasn't surprised when he got a note with
the name of a ship and a departure time. Just the name of the
ship and the sailing date, no appeal for him to come and say
goodbye. That choice was left up to him. But Loy also wrote:

Marry Nell and raise a family. You'll be a great father.
Teach your sons how to play football and cosy in those
corner kicks. You'll never join the Revolution so look out
for Number One.

Cosy checked the newspaper listings and saw that Loy's
ship, the *Ft. Saint George*, Furness Red Cross Line, was sailing
to New York To Pier 74, North River, Foot 34th Street, New
York City, the paper said. He tried for some time to imagine
what sailing into New York harbour would look like. On sailing day he went to work early, but he stayed away from his
company's docks, which were just to the west of those of
Harvey & Company, agents for the Red Cross Line. He
wouldn't allow himself even to look out his department's
third-floor windows at the harbour.

When the deep and mournful tuba-sound of the *Ft. Saint George*'s horn echoed off the South Side Hills Cosy stood very still. When the second series of blasts came, he moved. He bounded down the wide stairwell six steps at a time and pushed through the great revolving door. He sprinted along Water Street to Harvey's, then on through the terminal shed and out to the pier. The sun had not yet risen over the surrounding hills, but was streaming in through the Narrows. The *Ft. Saint George* was a stark silhouette, two hundred yards out, gliding toward the steep-sided gap.

He shielded his eyes from the sun and peered at the passengers lining the stern rail. Many of them were waving, but they were too small and he couldn't pick out Loy.

He wanted him to be there. He wanted Loy to see him.

His eyes were glistening with tears now. He didn't dare look at the other people on the pier. Most of them had stopped waving and were moving off to the terminal. Silently, he urged the remainder on.

Finally, he was alone. The *Ft. Saint George* was almost in the Narrows. Then, for the first time, he waved. He held a white handkerchief high over his head and slowly pulled it through the air in a graceful arc, back and forth, back and forth.

When the next war came and Nell's first child was six years old, Cosy was too old to go and fight. During those years, he often took the boy and his younger brother to the harbour to see the warships. He told them the story of how the Lone Eagle had waggled his wings at him before flying out through the Narrows to glory, and how he had met the Colonel at Bay Bulls Big Pond. (He never told them about Loy Fleming, though. Nor had he ever told Nell that for a while he had received some letters from Loy at his firm. The letters were sent from New York where Loy had landed a job on a newspaper; they were filled with excitement about the city and the stories he worked on. In his last letter Loy said he was off to cover a civil war in

Spain. Cosy never answered any of the letters. He felt he had nothing to tell.)

The boys were more interested in the warships than in Lindbergh. There were always dozens of them in the harbour, destroyers and frigates and corvettes, escort ships for the great North Atlantic convoys. Sometimes the ships limped in with jagged holes in their sleek grey hulls or their towering super-structures twisted and partly blown away. Cosy talked to the young sailors, invited them to his home. Some of them came back again and again between runs across the cruel U-boat-infested gauntlet to places such as Liverpool, and later Murmansk. Nell fed them home-cooked meals and the English ones called her Ma. But those friendships were painful. Cosy tried to shield his boys from worrying too much about the safety of the Harrys and Syds and Nigels that came to their home and played with them. But there always came a time when their grey ships slipped out through the Narrows in the cold pre-dawn light and off to the war beyond the horizon. You never knew if they were coming back.

At Jamie's bedtime that night his mother told him to say an extra special prayer for his Uncle Sid. "The poor man is worse," Ada Gosse said, and when Jamie asked if Uncle Sid was going to "pass away" like Albert Morton she shushed him and told him not to talk like that. Albert had disappeared from Jamie's fifth-grade class at school earlier that fall; it was explained to the boys that he had suddenly got sick and had passed away and gone to heaven to see God and get better. Jamie's Uncle Sid, on the other hand, had been sick for years from the wounds he had suffered in the first World War. And when it came that night to Uncle Sid's turn in his prayers, Jamie pictured behind his tightly squinched eyes the heavy guns on his uncle's wall, trophies of that war. They had been promised to him some day and he could see his hands reaching out for them.

Although the new war against Hitler was winding down, a full-scale blackout was still in effect in the port city of St. John's and Jamie's mother never let him out on the streets after dark. "How am I supposed to give that boy a decent upbringing," she complained to her husband. "Every night you've got drunken foul-mouthed sailors out on the street with foolish girls. Have you seen them? They're fornicating in public! Up against the telephone poles!" Lately, she said, she had even seen couples doing it in the daytime over in Parson's field where Jamie played football. Frank Gosse was an air-raid warden and Ada said that at least he could try to *do* something to help protect their son. Unlike his brother, Sid, Frank had been too young for the first great war, too old for the second. He had worked for years at the same job in one of the big stores on Water Street. When Jamie brought home his report card from school he always gave it to his mother, just as his father handed over his pay packet to her every Friday.

Jamie and his father had paid regular monthly visits to

Uncle Sid's house for some time; the first Saturday afternoon after starting his special prayer for his uncle, Jamie was particularly anxious to get there. Nobody ever used Uncle Sid's front door. Callers went around to the backyard and entered the house directly into the kitchen. When Jamie and his father arrived Uncle Sid was sitting as usual in his wide chair, surrounded by his vats for making homebrew. His blue parrot, Pol, shrieked, "Jamie's here—Jamie's here—Jamie's here." but this time, racing through the kitchen, Jamie ignored the parrot and his uncle's greeting, ignored Fergus, the tail-less dog whose only trick was to walk across the room on his hind legs, and the nameless spider mokey swinging from cold-water ceiling pipes. He finally stopped in the front hall at the place he had been thinking about all the way over. There, up on the wall over the stair landing, hung one above the other, were two Enfield .303s, bolt-action rifles with bayonets attached; below them was a German 9mm Mauser rifle, a bolt-action too, but no bayonet. Jamie took the Mauser down and lugged it back to the kitchen. He propped himself against the doorjamb, got the rifle up to his shoulder and sized up his uncle in the sights.

Uncle Sid was Jamie's favourite uncle, a huge, jolly man who had rings of fat like inner tubes around his middle. He weighed over three hundred pounds. On the rare occasion when he came to Jamie's house in winter they had to unbolt the double storm door to get him in. He had no neck and his great round head sat directly on his shoulders like a balloon with bumps on it for a chin and a nose, a thin slash of a line upcurved at the ends for a mouth, stuck on ears, and two little eye-holes like fire pits glowing with warm blue flame. His was a man-in-the-moon face, the laughing kind.

"You want me to croak quicker so you can get your hands on those guns?" Uncle Sid called out. "Go ahead. Shoot me."

"Don't point guns, Jamie!" his father said. "Accidents happen that way."

"Ah, leave him alone," Uncle Sid said. "It's never loaded.

Go ahead," he called to Jamie. "As long as you blow me a kiss before you pull the trigger."

"Jamie!" his father said.

Jamie ignored him. His father hadn't been in any wars at all. How could he know anything about guns? Besides, Uncle Sid said it wasn't loaded. And still sighting down the barrel of the Mauser, he could see now that Uncle Sid had changed because of his sickness, especially his surprising colour. He looked a bit smaller, and it was funny the way he was wearing one of his old army caps indoors, how it sat down over his ears. But his colour was the most startling change. He was kind of orange all over—his hands, his face, his ankles above his socks. Why? Jamie wondered, before he pressed the trigger, making a popping noise with his lips.

"Some kiss!" Uncle Sid exclaimed, clapping his one good arm to his chest as if wounded. "Come on over here now and give me a real one!"

The ingredients for Uncle Sid's homebrewed spruce beer lay on a battered wooden table beside his chair—bags of sugar, yeast, sticky balls of frankum, mounds of spruce buds. Stuck point down among the buds was the bayonet belonging to the German Mauser. Unlike the English bayonets, it was a black and vicious looking thing with a serrated upper edge which Uncle Sid said, "could really rip your belly up and spill your guts on the ground." Uncle Sid used the bayonet for everything, always had it with him.

Jamie touched the bayonet at the top of the handle and wiggled it. He glanced up at his uncle. "Why are you so orange, Uncle Sid? Because you're sick?"

His father jumped in quickly. "Uncle Sid's got to take a special medicine, Jamie. It changes the colour of his skin for a while. That's all."

"That's all?" Uncle Sid echoed loudly. "Shit! I wish the name of Christ it *was* all, Frank. Look at this!" And he lifted his forage cap and Jamie saw that he was completely bald.

36

That was what had made him look so funny—he had no side-burns under the hat.

"I shaved it clean because the hair was falling out," Uncle Sid said. "This goddam thing is eating me up so quick there's gonna be nothing left for the worms when I get to my grave."

"C'mon Sid!" Jamie's father whined. "There're some things Ada doesn't think we should talk about yet in front of him." He jerked his head at Jamie. "You know what I mean."

Jamie wiggled the bayonet free and slid it along the table to Uncle Sid's chair. He touched his uncle's arm. "Uncle Sid. Tell me again the story about how you got the Mauser from the German...*Please.*"

The parrot shrieked, "Please—Pretty please—Please—Pretty please—Please..."

"Oh shut up, Pol," Uncle Sid yelled, throwing his cap at the bird. Overhead, spotting his uncovered dome, the nameless monkey came swinging swiftly down a pipe on the wall, leapt across to the back of Uncle Sid's chair and started running its tiny fingers over his scalp.

"Get the fuck off me!" Uncle Sid shouted, swiping at the monkey with his good arm. "I haven't got any hair anymore so fuck off!"

Jamie, laughing, grabbed for the monkey too, yelling for it to fuck off, fuck off, fuck off. But the animal streaked through the air from the back of Uncle Sid's chair to the pipe on the wall and up to safety. Then Jamie's father collared him and clipped him on the back of the head. Jamie was expecting a bawling out, but instead his father started complaining to Uncle Sid. How could he blame the boy, he said, when he heard that kind of language from his uncle. He knew that Sid was in pain, he went on, but Jesus, if Ada heard the boy saying fuck this and fuck that she'd say in a flash that he had picked it up from his uncle and that would be the end of these visits.

First Uncle Sid looked hurt, then he got angry. "Goddamit, Frank! There're not gonna be many more visits...and stop sounding so shit-scared of Ada. She lets the boy come over here like I was some kind of victim on the dole and she was giving me handouts. She's got you by the short and curlies, Frank. I told you before you married her that she was stuck up. She thinks she's better than we are and you're letting her turn that boy into a pansy. Right now she wouldn't let him say shit if his mouth was full of it."

Jamie giggled. Uncle Sid didn't sound sick at all when he was like this. But suddenly he looked sick. He was sweating and he slumped back in his chair and covered his face with his hand. Then, after a moment, he muttered okay, he'd wash his mouth out, but no soap and water. Frank had to draw them a couple of glasses of brew. And when he lowered his hand his great orange moonface was grinning mischievously. "Do you still want to hear that story?" he asked.

Once again Uncle Sid told them about the morning of the fourteenth of April, 1917, in a place called Monchy. Supposed to be a beautiful old French town, he said, but it was an old dump by the time the Regiment arrived. A lot of heavy fighting had torn the place apart, nobody had time to bury the dead and they didn't look very nice.

"And boy, the smell!" He pinched his nostrils and tilted his big head back and went "Phee-ew!"

His company went straight into the frontline trenches at dusk, he said, and spent the night before the attack among the rotting corpses. The next morning they waited for the whistle to go over the top and some of the men were praying and some were throwing up and some just wanted to get out of the stink even if it meant they had to face the German machine guns. He stuck out his good arm and swept it across the kitchen—"Rat-tat-tat-tat-tat"—and stopped at the end of the arc he made to take the glass of pale-yellow spruce beer that Jamie's father was holding out to him.

"I was orderly for Captain Dick Curran, M.C., Military Cross," he said. "Like a brother to me Curran was. Best Captain in the Regiment." He paused, swallowed some beer, then sniffed and wiped at his broad face, his eyes and nose. He looked at his brother. "You remember Dick Curran, Frank? God, he was one hell of a man."

And Jamie's father, a man who considered himself deeply unfortunate, both in his own eyes and in those of others, to have missed both wars, nodded respectfully in the silence, even though he had heard this story a dozen times.

"Get to the part with the big German," Jamie urged, leaning on the arm of his uncle's chair.

Uncle Sid stared at him blankly for a moment. White drool ran down a crease in his jowls from the corner of his mouth, but he ignored it and said, "Okay, okay, but don't rush me." Then he drew a deep breath, sighed and began again.

So it was eight o'clock on the morning of the fourteenth, he said, when they went over the top. He was by Captain Curran's side and the next thing he knew the Captain went to his knees and clutched at his chest, blood spurting out of him in a jet. He clapped his hand to his own fat chest as if stanching a wound or taking an oath. "The best and bravest man I knew," he said, "and a bullet got him in the lung." He paused as if it were an official moment of silence, then looked at Jamie and said, "Saved my life though, he did."

Next he told how he'd been bent over his Captain and tending to his wound when the Captain said watch out Sid. And he spun around to the front just in time to see this big Hun lunging at him with his bayonet. He had time to shift a bit, he said, and the bayonet went between his side and his arm, catching a piece of the flesh inside his bicep. He patted his useless arm, the same one that was later ripped apart by machine-gun bullets all the way up through his shoulder. Blood was streaming down his tunic, he said, making his hand all wet, but he grabbed the German's Mauser by the barrel and held on. Like this, he said, putting down his beer and clamping his good arm tight to his side, his hand stuck out in front like a claw, clutching at the imaginary rifle barrel. He looked at Jamie. "Now the dirty bugger couldn't pull back and shoot me, you

39

see, and he saw that I had him dead." So what did the Hun do? Well he let go of that Mauser, he said, and he turned and ran. But he wasn't as fast as your Uncle Sid, who tore his arm free from the bayonet, picked up the Mauser, and stuck the brute in the back of the neck with his own bloody saw-toothed knife. He paused dramatically, staring hard at Jamie. "And it came right out through the bugger's eye and he was as dead as a doornail."

Jamie held up the German bayonet and Uncle Sid nodded. "That's it. The very one." And Jamie said, "Yes, I know, but listen. You promised I could have the guns but this is never on the Mauser. Now that you're sick can I have this too when you pass away?"

"Jamie!" his father said sharply. "You're not to talk like that!"

Uncle Sid chuckled, shaking his massive head. "You can have it when it's time you little conniver," he said, holding out his hand for the bayonet. He looked at the wall clock. "Right now I need some *Swish* for when the boys get here, so how about it. Go roll some barrels around out back and earn yourself ten cents."

While he could still get around, Uncle Sid had been a night watchman at the Navy Dockyard down on the harbour. Jamie believed he was guarding against German spies and saboteurs, but the job was make-work, really, a sinecure created for a disabled veteran who sat around all night in a shack, drinking and talking and bartering with the visiting sailors. That was how he had acquired the parrot and the monkey. The Dockyard was also a storage place for empty wooden rum barrels. Affable Sid had arranged to have a number of them delivered to his backyard each week. Jamie's ten-cent job was to put a little hot water in through the bungholes of the barrels from a tap at the back of the house, then roll them around the yard. That was what Uncle Sid called "swishing out the rum." And the drink that got poured from the barrels into bottles he called *Swish*.

Now, Jamie went "swishing" while his father crossed the yard to pay his respects to Uncle Sid's wife who ran a small confectionery shop that fronted on the next block. Aunt Norma was a childless woman who, in Jamie's view, was really tight with her candy, claiming that she was only obeying the rules that Jamie's mother had laid down for his visits. Jamie was kicking a barrel about the yard, Fergus barking and scampering around his feet, when he heard the voices of the men from the Regiment. They spilled from the laneway around the corner of the house, the tall one, Captain Leo Malloy, shepherding the others up the steps to the kitchen door. Their voices cried out to him:

"Kick the arse off her, Jamie!"

"Put the bloody boots to her lad!"

"No friggin in the bunghole, Jamie boy!"

Jamie glanced at Aunt Norma's shop, knowing he had only a few minutes. For it was always the said: whenever the men from the Regiment arrived and the fun really started, his father and he quickly departed.

He ran up to the kitchen door and went inside.

The men were laughing and joking and the room was already filling with cigarette smoke. He pushed through to Uncle Sid's chair and whispered about his dime and waited until he got it. Then he saw his father standing in the door looking for him. He knew he should go to his father but he lingered. Captain Malloy and his men had to know.

"You're the officer here, Leo," a voice called to Captain Malloy. "Get a detail together and get that fucking *Swish* in here toot sweet."

"Yeah, Leo. Move your fucking *derrière*."

The cursing drew Jamie's father farther into the crowded room. He looked uncomfortable among the veterans.

Jamie darted across to Captain Malloy. He got the tall officer's smiling attention and blurted quickly, "Uncle Sid says his guns and bayonets, even his special Mauser bayonet, you know, the one he killed the German with..." He caught his breath. "Well he says they're all mine when he passes away and you're to tell the others..."

Captain Malloy's smile stiffened, then vanished. He jerked his head at the door. "Why don't you piss off home with your father kid. Your uncle ain't ready for the bugler yet."

Startled, Jamie backed up and bumped into his father.

"Sorry, Leo," his father said with a nervous grin. "Come on Jamie. Time to go." And he tried to take Jamie's hand, but Jamie pushed him away and ran out the kitchen door.

Before another month had passed Jamie was back in his Uncle Sid's kitchen, this time for his wake. His parents had disagreed about him going there, but his father had insisted. "Listen to me Ada!" he had said with uncharacteristic vehemence. "One of the last times I talked to Sid he said we were turning the boy into a pansy and I think he was right. We're protecting him too much." Sid loved the boy, he said, and he would have wanted him there. Ada, surprised by Frank's outburst, had given in on one condition—she didn't want Jamie looking at any corpse.

Jamie was scrubbed and brushed and dressed up in his long flannels and blazer, white shirt and school tie, just like when he went to church or to a party—except for the black armband his father had pinned on his sleeve. For him the wake *seemed* like a party and that puzzled him. It had been sad at school when Albert Morton had "passed away," yet everybody here was celebrating. Uncle Sid meant far more to him than Albert and he had been really sad when his mother told him that he would never see his uncle again in this life. But here the noisy people crowded into the kitchen and out into the hallway sounded happy. The men from the Regiment were drinking and telling funny stories about Uncle Sid. Captain Malloy told one that he swore he'd seen with his own eyes about how Sid was carrying a bucket of water back to the trenches when a shell exploded nearby. "He went straight up in the air with his bucket and turned arse over kettle and when he came down he landed on his own two feet and he hadn't spilled a drop. That's not a word of a lie, so help me God." The men all laughed a lot, but unlike during the old Saturday afternoon visits they minded their language. That, Jamie figured, was because of his mother and the other women present.

The look of the kitchen—all cleaned up—had startled Jamie. Uncle Sid's beer vats and all his fixings were gone. But what concerned him most was the absence of Pol and the nameless monkey—only Fergus remained, out in the backyard now with the *Swish* barrels. He asked his father where the animals had gone and was told that Aunt Norma didn't have time to look after them and had to give them away. That upset him, and then he began to wonder if Aunt Norma had done something with the guns too. And the German bayonet? It wasn't on the table! Maybe Aunt Norma had the guns over in her store and was going to sell them. Maybe she had given them already to Captain Malloy and the Regiment.

He looked at the tall officer across the kitchen, but he was afraid to go up to him again and ask. And neither could he go into the hallway to look at the wall over the landing and see if the guns were still there because his mother had warned him strictly to stay in the kitchen. By now, he had worked himself into a state about his guns and he had to know.

Aunt Norma, he learned by asking, was in the front room where Uncle Sid was laid out. Those two words puzzled him. Uncle Sid, his mother had said, had "passed away" and there would be a nice funeral and he would go to heaven, just like Albert Morton. So what was he doing "laid out" in the front room? Earlier, he had wondered about the word "wake" too. Why were they having a "wake" for Uncle Sid? What did that mean? His mother had explained that it was just a ceremony to honour his uncle. But now he heard one of the women who had just come in from the front room tell his mother that Uncle Sid looked lovely, "just like he was asleep," and he thought for moment about his uncle literally *waking* up and joining the party. But that, he knew, wasn't possible once you'd "passed away."

He told his mother he was going out to the yard to play with Fergus and she warned him not to get his good clothes dirty. Once outside, he raced around the side of the house to the front door—it had been opened up for the wake and for the funeral the next day. People were milling about in the front hallway, though it wasn't as crowded as the kitchen. A woman, sobbing into a handkerchief, came out of the living-room. He heard a man next to him say it was cancer of the gullet, that Uncle Sid had starved to death in no time at all. "It's a sad thing to see," another man replied, "but we all gotta die someday, I suppose."

One quick look at the wall above the stair landing had told Jamie that his guns were safe. But he didn't leave. What lay beyond the door to the living-room had a scary fascination for him now that made him forget the guns and drew him on. Just at the doorjamb the sudden, sickly sweet and cloying odour of decaying flowers swamped his nostrils and his throat. He didn't want to breathe, but he had to look.

Inside, a box of dark, shiny wood with brass handles sat on a low table that was draped with purple cloth. Aunt Norma was seated at the head of the box, dressed completely in black and with a black veil over her face. A man was standing over her, murmuring some words of comfort. Others stood behind him, waiting their turn. Banks of flowered wreaths were piled around the walls of the room.

Then, jutting just above the rim of the box at Aunt Norma's end, Jamie saw a face, rigid like a mask, eyes closed. He felt the shock of recognition tingle on his skin. It was Uncle Sid. Much thinner, but definitely Uncle Sid. He wasn't orange anymore. He was white. A pale, waxy white. And he wasn't asleep and he wasn't in heaven. He was something else…

Jamie's original feeling of sadness about losing Uncle Sid turned at that moment to one of terror over what had

44

happened to him—his change into that creepy body. And trembling with fear he fled to the kitchen and to his mother.

Later that night, sitting at Jamie's bedside and comforting him, his mother explained that the real Uncle Sid, his soul, was no longer in the body that Jamie had seen in the box, but somewhere up above, looking down on them all, smiling. Jamie stared up at her with wide-eyed intensity, clinging to her words. But when his mother left and he closed his eyes to sleep, he saw again the pale white corpse lying in the casket.

The Reverend Charley Brinton, The Regiment's old chaplain, stood in the fresh dirt at the head of the grave, his Book of Common Prayer raised up close to his eyes. Jamie stood next to his father at the other end, his eyes red from rubbing at them. Corporal Sid Gosse's coffin, draped in the Union Jack, rested on straps above a deep hole with pools of muddy brown water at the bottom.

The Reverend Brinton intoned, "I am the resurrection and the life, saith the Lord: he that believeth in me, though he were dead, yet shall he live: and whosoever liveth and believeth in me shall never die."

After what had happened at the wake, Ada hadn't wanted her son to go to the funeral and Jamie didn't want to go either. But again his father had insisted that his Uncle Sid would have wanted it that way. "Besides," Frank said, "Jamie is old enough now to start behaving like a man." Puzzled as to what he meant by that, Ada had relented for the second time in 48 hours in the face of her husband's new-found forcefulness. The funeral itself was unusual. Corporal Sid Gosse considered the high point of his life to have been the time he had spent long ago in a war-time trench in France with his buddies and he wanted his complete funeral service held at the graveside—"the next best thing to a trench I know," he'd said. The procession, therefore, bypassed the cathedral where the Regiment's colours hung and went directly from Sid's house to the cemetery. The men of the Regiment, "the old comrades" they called

themselves, proudly wore their uniforms, including their
famous blue puttees, and marched behind the horse-drawn
hearse. Jamie and his father were at the head of the procession,
and Jamie couldn't avoid looking at the coffin inside the glass-
walled and silver-trimmed hearse that swayed silently on its
rubber wheels. He started snivelling the moment the coffin
left Uncle Sid's house and they had left his mother and the
other women behind. He walked more than two miles, holding his father's hand and hating it. Ever since Uncle Sid had
died his father had changed, but he could never be one of
Uncle Sid's real friends like the men of the Regiment. Jamie
had seen proof of that with the way Captain Leo Malloy and
the others had treated his father.

The Reverend Brinton lowered his book and stepped aside
carefully to make room for Captain Malloy to come forward to
the head of the grave and deliver the eulogy. A steady bank of
fog had been hanging along the back side of Signal Hill and
sheets of it started tearing away from the edges, drifting up
along Quidi Vidi pond, wisping across the shoreline and the
cemetery. Soon, Jamie could barely make out the honour
guard. Their guns were .303 Enfields, the same as the ones on
Uncle Sid's wall. But in his misery he no longer cared about
the guns or what Captain Malloy was saying. He was thinking
about his mother and how she would punish his father. Right
now she was probably in the warm kitchen, baking things in
the big stove and getting supper ready for when they got
home, and when they did he would tell her how much he had
hated the funeral. She would let his father eat his supper, probably even let him read his paper a bit in front of the fire, waiting until it was time for him, Jamie, to go up to bed. After that
she would scold his father without pity and tell him he should
never make his son do something like this again. And his
father would drop his paper on the floor and lean his elbows on
his knees and hunch his shoulders and put his head down the
way he always did when she scolded him about his job and
money and things and he had none of the right answers.

When the first rifle reports cracked in the thickening fog, Jamie jumped with fright. And when a bugle started sounding the last post the notes were eerie and muffled. Jamie couldn't see the buglar, but he could see that the coffin was beginning to sink slowly into the dark hole in the earth. The trees overhanging the plot were dripping water now and he shuddered from the wet and the cold. He sniffed and felt the sobs that would rack his body stirring in him again. He wanted to go home to his mother. At the same time, however, he couldn't take his eyes off the box going down and down into that dank horrifying hole, the voice of the Reverend Brinton intoning in the fog:

"Forasmuch as it hath pleased Almighty God of his great mercy to receive unto himself the soul of our dear brother here departed: we therefore commit his body to the ground; earth to earth, ashes to ashes, dust to dust; in sure and certain hope of the Resurrection to eternal life..."

Jamie went to bed early that night with a runny nose, his mother concerned that he had caught a chill at the cemetery. She listened to the hurried rote of his prayers, then attempted soothing answers to his worried questions about sealed-up coffins and muddy graves. When she went downstairs she left his door open, the upstairs hall light on.

Soon after that, when he heard the indistinct but angry sound of his mother's voice rising from below, Jamie crept out in the hall and sat on the floor by the bannisters overlooking the staircase. As he had fancied at the cemetery she was indeed scolding his father, blaming him for the awful things the funeral had done to her boy.

"Stop it, Ada!" his father suddenly shouted. "Stop it right now!"

There was silence for a moment. Then Jamie heard a sound he'd never heard before, the sound of his father crying.

"Oh, Frank, Frank, don't cry," his mother said in her quiet soothing voice. "I'm so sorry you feel like that... It's my fault

47

I've..." Her voice broke, catching on a sob. "I've been so selfish with him, I know...but I never meant to hurt you." Then she was crying softly and his father was comforting her, murmuring that it wasn't her fault.

Later, in the middle of the night, Jamie had a bad dream in which he was down in a dark muddy trench with rotting corpses. Uncle Sid's German was among them, the ugly saw-toothed bayonet sticking out through his eye. In the dream he was trying to climb out of the trench but kept sliding back, and he awoke struggling with his bedclothes. His room was pitch black—the hall light had been turned out—and he imagined himself inside a coffin like Uncle Sid, sinking into a hole in the earth.

He knew if he got up and turned on his own light or the hall light his mother would call out or come to his room. He didn't want that. And it was in that instant while thinking about his mother that an afterthought came to him like a sharp piercing arrow: his mother would die too. His mother would be a corpse like Uncle Sid. And his father too. They would not be here forever.

Panic drove Jamie from his bed to the window to tear aside the blackout shutter. Outside, the fog and drizzle had cleared off. It was the first real winter night of the year, crystal-clear, with a brilliant alabaster moon riding high above a scattered handful of clouds. A submariner's moon, the sailors called it, the light reflecting on the surface of the harbour and the sea outside in the cold merciless sheen that silhouetted their ships and made them easy prey for the U-Boat wolfpacks. The moonlight also made dark humps of the hills surrounding the harbour, cut sharp shadows on the city's dormant streets. And streaming now through Jamie's window, it bathed his pale uplifted face and filled his bedroom with a ghostly blue aura.

ELISE LEVINE

Angel

It was midnight, Angel, and I'll never forget. We did it in doorways up and down Church Street, my back against rotting wood or my hamstrings hurting, crouched down on grey concrete, the club where I'd cruised you receding as we twisted down alleyways and across half-empty parking-lots. You wooed me that night and I could hear my breath whistling in and out of me and when you pulled my shirt up and over my head and tossed it—just like that, in the middle of the street—it was like a ghost floated up inside me and fluttered out of my mouth, my white shirt sailing up over Parliament Street, and the next morning I saw it lying on the streetcar tracks at Queen and Sherbourne.

We were already light years away from everything I thought I knew—I was fresh off the bus from Owen Sound—and we never stopped once, skidding through the rain-slick streets of Rosedale at three in the morning or standing under the fluorescent hum of all-night pizza joints, hungry (we were so hungry). Or the night you turned a trick and next morning we took the Bathurst bus to Starkman's Surgical Supplies. You gave me the guided tour, row upon immaculate row of enema equipment, the smell of the rubber gloves you pressed to my face, and the shiny steel clamp you bought for $70. That night you pierced my right nipple—for love, you said, as I handed you the surgical steel ring—and that photographer documented it, then threw us out when we ripped through her cupboard for food.

I had walked into the city, Angel.

I never looked back.

Farmers were torching peaches in the Golden Horseshoe that summer. They were substandard—too small—and they smelled overripe and bursting with a faint odour of gasoline underneath and we lived on them for a month because they

cost next to nothing. I sold some blow in the bars and bought
a beat-up Chevy Nova for $500, and we'd drive it out of the
city to where it was dry and dusty, the late-August fields burning with goldenrod. We'd stop on dirt roads and my eyelids
would sweat as I squinted against the two o'clock sun, and
when you kissed me I remembered how it felt when you
pushed the needle through the cork and carefully threaded the
ring through me and I didn't flinch, only squeezed my eyes
half-shut against the pain and flushed cold-hot.

That's when you were there for me most, saying, Your aure-
ole, aurora, bright aura burning pink-gold; and the single
bead of blood below my nipple made me think of my heart
beating fast and clear underneath.

We'd drive real slow through Stouffville, then stop at
Musselmans' Lake to swim. And when you laid me on my
stomach in the grass it was like when I was fifteen at Kim
Evans' place at Swallow Lake and Leslie and I left the party and
kissed for the first time and I didn't want to go back up to the
cottage—the guys spraying beer at each other, Janet and Paul
locking themselves in Kim's parents' bedroom—but Leslie
cried and said she loved me but she was too afraid, she said,
This is wrong, and, David'll be looking for me, We're going
to get caught, she was so afraid of getting caught. Only now *I*
was afraid of getting caught, I knew the bikers at Musselmans'
could be pretty rough trade and I knew exactly what they
might do but we did it anyway, we always did it anyway.

And that was a little like what happened with Nancy Smith
and me when we were sixteen and we did it anyway and paid
the price, Lezzie cunt scratched on my locker at school and the
night I drove my Dad's car to the Esso off Main and Ken Hale
and his older brother and their friends were there, standing
around their pickups and Camaros and I felt a little nervous
but I got out of the car and walked over to the pump and took
down the hose and slowly unscrewed the gas cap and very carefully filled the tank but out of the corner of my eye I could see
one of the guys rubbing his dick and when he saw me notice

him he said, Look at her look, she knows I've got what she needs, and then I very carefully put the hose back but by then they were all walking over to me and saying things so I got in the car real quick and slammed the door shut and drove off, I never stopped to pay the bill, just made a fast left out of there and it wasn't till I was half-way down Main Street that I smelled the gas and realized I'd dropped the gas cap at the station and I was spilling tracks all the way down Main that night.

But you and me always did it anyway, Angel, and in the evening we'd drive back along the 400 doing a cool 140 K, slipping in and out of one long stream of tail-lights past Barrie, the long ride home like the strong fluid lines of a game of pool I'd seen you play one Saturday night in July at the old Cameo Club off Eastern Avenue. You'd just started taking me around, and the bouncer at the door that night had wanted to see my ID but you said, It's okay, Val, and she hissed, Baby dyke, at me under her breath and let me pass. You racked up those balls like a pro and beat those old dykes in their black leather vests who lovingly took their handcrafted, mother-of-pearl-inlaid cues from monogrammed cases and everyone stood around, and I counted each sudden click as you knocked the balls down, always where you said you wanted them and it was like each click that night brought me closer to something, each click a notch cut closer through the tension thick as the blue smoky bar or the heavenly sweet smell of amyl in the bathroom, and looking up I could see the smooth moves shaking it out there on the dance floor, but all I could hear was you, calling, Six ball in the corner pocket, and click, Nine ball in the side pocket, and all night long I felt I was moving, Angel, really moving.

It was like you were some kind of angel from outerspace, and I was strung out on some serious religious songs like your heart had all this voodoo over me. But you became featherlight; and in what became that wet summer city at night—the bars emptying—you had left hours earlier with someone else, and the streetlights seemed leprous, yellow like old age and neglect, like bright nimbuses of neglect.

Remember when we stole that van? Coked up and joyriding the 401 at four in the morning, we thought we'd get as far as Montreal then ditch the sucker. You were driving so fast, bouncing us between semis, each one carrying a single cargo of cowboy hurtling through the tail-end of a four-day run and I was riding fast and scared, a little slick between my legs and you were talking non-stop, saying we'd do this and then that, adventures, always big adventures and when you rolled the van a little ways out past Kingston I just held on tight and never screamed once.

Now I'm here in this hospital, Angel, because (forgive me) I tried to let you go. Three days ago they pumped my stomach, its shiny stinking freight of 200 assorted Christmas Trees and Percodans. Now they send round the therapists and social workers, the students from Abnormal Psych. 101 and there are things they want to hear but I know it's what they think they already know so I squeeze my eyes tight in concentration and I tell them nothing. *Queer girl*.

And this nothing but this light in my head.

So touch me. Touch me before I die of old age. I'm out on the streetcorner and the light haloes me and I'm waiting for you with my young lean body, its barely learned distrust of strangers.

So this is how I think of you, Angel.

The van's on fire and we're sitting in the ditch watching and I can feel the hot breath of escape on my face. You stand up and sway slightly from the effort then you walk out onto the shoulder and keep on going. And although I never see you again I'm still waiting by the side of the 401, waiting through the hot sting of freezing rain or the claustral breath of August and as each car screams past I lift my head to look for you, but it's never you, Angel. Never you.

But sometimes I think maybe you're here with me now, only we're out there, joyriding the lights glowing blue-black on wet summer streets or else we're driving easy with the windows down all the way and we're counting car headlights strung like pearls across the highway, and I keep thinking there's a city here somewhere but sometimes I find it a struggle to believe—but I do believe, Angel, I swear I do—and it's like I can almost see lights rocking across a harbour while the round earth's rocking and calling to us, and it's funny but I can remember being in the back seat of a car when I was really little and being rocked to sleep by the motion, and right now I can feel the top of my skull nasty and bubbling with amphetamines. And yours too, sure, yours too.

Back There

Janis peeled off her stretch-denim pants. Sassy, and smart—that's what Janis' mother had called them last fall when she placed the order by phone from the Sears catalogue, along with matching stretch-denim shorts, a hip-length jacket with a long pointy collar, even a stretch-denim poncho; though Janis had her doubts when, wearing the pants and jacket, she called for her best friend Monica on the first day of school and Monica's brother turned from the door to yell, Monica—Lumpy's here.

Now it was summer. For two days Janis and her mother had been sitting around the swimming-pool at the airport Holiday Inn in Montreal studying the bathing-suits and perfect bodies of Lufthansa stewardesses while Janis' father attended Expo ball games. To Janis' mother, originally from New Brunswick, this was the high life. She'd always wanted to travel.

On the third day Janis' mother insisted on a morning bus tour of downtown, with stops along St. Catherine for shopping. Too many choices, her mother kept saying, avidly circling the shoe departments: the pink vinyl or the white strappy sandals? She finally settled on the pale blue runners.

Worse, there were sheets and shams and tasseled things. Janis agreed: too many choices. She couldn't wait to get back to the pool.

In the hotel-room Janis pulled on her terry-cloth bathing-suit and ran outside. From above the pool was a rectangle of light that levitated unsettlingly; she grasped the balcony railing for a second, woozy, sheer height lapping at her ankles.

Janis' mother joined her and together they lodged themselves in chairs on the pool deck. The women were out in full force: several at a patio table, ordering drinks from the waiter; two sunning themselves, artfully arranged elegant as dolls, swapping copies of *Der Spiegel* and *Elle*; and one in the shallow end of the pool, laughing, splashing water on her arms and tanned breasts, yipping sweetly at the cold.

Janis' mother surveyed the gingham bathing suits with white flounces, the plaid Sea Queen, the floral "Goddess" by Gottex (she had lingered over the same suit that morning at The Bay, she whispered proudly to Janis). Janis sensed her mother longed for clothes the way men longed for women—smoulderingly—in the old movies Janis wasn't supposed to see but did, creeping down the stairs late at night to sit just outside the living-room doorway while inside her parents watched TV.

Janis herself longed for nailpolish; it was the one reason she could give for wanting to grow up. Around her the women's extremities looked like fields of poppies waving slightly from the barest blush of a breeze.

After what seemed like hours, one of the women leaned forward in her *chaise-longue*. She swung her legs around to one side and stood, towering blondly over Janis and her mother. The woman looked down and smiled at Janis. Janis' mother smiled back. Everyone, it seemed, was smiling, into the bright sunshine.

Janis, her mother said. It's time I tell you about something.

Janis soon stopped listening. Airplanes flew low in the sky. Her eyes hurt from looking at the pool. The highway beyond the chain-fence rattled, something a baby might shake from time to time. She looked down at her body, laid out before her, plump, sunburned pink as a salmon at the Holiday Inn's lunchtime buffet table.

She looked about in desperation for something to throw over herself.

She longed for her poncho.

Fifteen years later Janis watched her mother in the swimming-pool at the Lewiston, New York motel—a woman terrified, much of her life, of the water though she had been taking a weekly Beginner Aquafit class for years. Through half-shut eyes Janis watched her mother in the shallow end. She held on to the side of the pool with both hands and bounced up and down, closing her eyes in concentration and forming an *o* with her mouth. Clearly, Janis thought, the classes had helped.

Boy that feels good.

Water sprinkled Janis' face and arms, waking her. Don't stand so close, she said, clenching her teeth, a wad of molar and cuspid lodged deep in her mouth.

Janis that sun's nice isn't it. Janis' mother lay back in a *chaise-longue*. Janis fell asleep again. She dreamed she was on a beach in Cuba, far, far away. She was happy. But then farmers burned the sugar cane and the insects came. She woke up furious. She read Smollet; she read Austen. She was bored, tired. Her mother sat on the edge of her *longue*, smoking, smoking.

Later that afternoon Janis wanted to die: to rise up out of the red three-button Henley her mother bought her at The Gap and leave it flapping in the dust, dust of dusts. Janis, her mother said. Isn't this smart. Janis stood by helplessly as her mother ordered up outfit after outfit, as if it were her job though she had stopped working years ago when she became pregnant with Janis. I'll try that in a medium, she demanded repeatedly, no matter how form-clinging, her round stomach bulging through elegant knitwear beneath a rayon vest, black and ivory diamonds.

Only a hundred and fifteen.

Janis stood so still she almost forgot to breathe. Snob! her mother cried after the shrinking saleshelp—busy, busy with other customers, with the cash register, busy with anything— who could hear, of course they could hear.

Up, Janis thought, the red shirt like earth dourly clinging to her hands, her feet. She knew if she looked down, she'd see her body white as salt beneath her.

In J.C. Penney's they argued over intimate apparel. Janis' mother—who still used words such as *sizzle* and *pizzazz*—admired the denim-look Guess underwire bras with matching panties; Janis insisted on the black and magenta Gitano, trimmed with lace.

Wear it yourself, Janis finally said and stared at her mother who grasped the Guess bra on its hanger. I need more support, her mother said. She replaced the hanger on the rack. But I'd love to. I'd love to.

You're young, Janis' mother said over coffee, her styrofoam cup kissed by lipstick. You can wear anything.

That night they went to hear Ella Fitzgerald in concert, her sequined voice faintly numinous, Janis thought, like a sighting of silver through midnight trees, shot through with shivery greens and golds. After the concert, Janis stood outside the pavillion, breathing slowly into a night flush with cicadas. A crescent moon was rising. She waited for her mother to reach the exit and locate her in the crowd. She didn't like being up so high, waiting like this; she wished her mother would hurry up so they could leave.

A dream, Janis.

Her mother was talking to her, though still a great distance below, trapped amid the leisurely exodus from rows P to T.

Janis wasn't she just a dream?

Janis looked down at her mother, her moss-green linen suit a barest glimmer, like a memory. Janis knew years from now her mother would remember the event by what she'd been wearing. She saved everything, ardently: a pink cocktail dress, hot pants, *her* mother's fox fur collar dark as loam in the cedar chest. That way, she once told Janis, she'd lose nothing. Besides, she like to say, what goes around comes around. You might want them someday.

Janis stepped away, higher up the hill then caught herself and stopped.

Janis?

Heads turned. Her mother was almost talking to herself.

Boy how old do you think she is she must be getting on.

Janis' breath streamed into the cooling air. The light flutter in her jeans caught her by surprise, wafting up to hold her, briefly, fiercely, by the throat. Tension, she thought. Butterflies. Though not quite the same as before. Now the jeans were looser, back to normal. Everything was back to normal, except for the occasional spotting—like the tension, a residue only.

She'd almost forgotten, had put it out of her mind.

Her mother caught up with her. Janis wasn't she just a dream, her mother was saying.

The next morning Janis wore the red shirt her mother bought her. They walked along a paved path on the American side of the Falls; Janis listened for its spin in her ears. She tried to keep her eye on her mother—always right up to the edge, leaning over the green railing. Janis! her mother called, and pointed.

We could try the Alpine ride.

Janis stopped and stared at her mother who stopped too, and looked out at the water and sky. Behind her mother's head Janis could see cables slung like tightropes from which, at regular intervals, tiny green cars dangled. From this distance they looked like toys. Janis thought she could see movement in one: two small figures at the top of the windy world, arms waving; they could almost be shouting, she thought, to make themselves heard over the wind, the wind itself pushing the shouting into their doll-like bodies, past dull wooden throats into bellies big as balloons. Janis half-expected them to float out the car window and rise, and never stop.

No way, Janis said to her mother. Not in a million years. Not on your life.

Janis' mother waited for Janis to start walking again. Behind her left shoulder Janis heard her mother say, You're no fun.

On their way home they crossed the border at the Rainbow Bridge. All around cars hummed lazy as bees. Silver Accord. White Aerostar. Red LeBaron, top down. Janis and her mother in the Buick: almost through, after half an hour jammed into a line of cross-border shoppers. The Accord hovered briefly then floated away. Aerostar. LeBaron: nice-looking guy in RayBans.

Janis. That line looks faster.

LeBaron removed his RayBans, dreamily wagging his dimples at the customs officer who waved him on. Gone, Janis thought, shifting from neutral to first. Bastard. Beside her, her mother was scratching her hands, one at a time. She twisted her wedding ring around on her finger. She had never learned to drive. Janis, she said, strangely plaintive. Janis. Janis rolled down her window and pulled alongside the booth. Janis she looks mean, her mother whispered, then leaned forward to smile toothily, like a dangerous animal, at the officer.

Toronto—St. John, Janis and her mother said at the same time in reply to the officer's question. Then they waited. Integra-Sunbird-Civic behind them, a shining Supreme at the booth to the right: all that metal and exhaust sticky as gum, stuck to the asphalt, a congealed trail reaching back for miles into a promised land of discount malls, cheap Levis, the candy-apple-reddest sunhats a heart could desire. Janis figured it didn't matter where you came from—no Canadian could resist.

The officer nodded.

As Janis pulled away from the booth her mother rubbed her hands together. Boy that was close.

Why'd you buy so much? Janis snapped.

Her mother smiled serenely. It gives me a lift, she said.

Two hours later Janis drove her father's Buick over the Burlington Skyway. The wind nosed the car slightly to the left side of the lane; a moment later, to the right. Her neck hurt.

She glanced past her lane: sky blue as blown glass, the lake below industrial but wide all the way back to suburban Buffalo, to Tonawanda and Lackawanna. From high school history class she knew these were Iroquois names, that Toronto was Huron; to Janis they had always been tracts of land blank as textbooks. Only the fires were memorable: always a fire in Tonawanda, according to the Channel 7 Eyewitness newscast out of Buffalo every Friday night before the late-show when Janis was small. After the fire came either the Mummy, ancient and only vaguely Egyptian, or King Kong, locked gamely in the arms of an impassioned Godzilla. The station was also famous for displaying the sign, "Do You Know Where Your Children Are?" during commercial breaks. Janis' mother always sat up with her and watched.

At the bridge's apex the pitch and shudder grew worse. Janis concentrated on the road so hard she thought her neck might break and her head roll off, glass-eyed and hard as porcelain. She could see her mother breathe, and breathe and stop, each time holding her breath as if (it seemed to Janis) she thought she could will her daughter—poppet, small bleating thing—to the Skyway despite the absolute lure and spin of the world.

Stop it.

Her mother jumped. What? she said. What did I do now?

Janis wanted to stretch, to ease her head to the left, to slowly count eight seconds before carefully turning her head to the right.

What.

The wide view stretching below, above—land seeping into sky—impossibly septic from industry, history, from everything that had ever happened. Janis wanted to point, chatter uncontrollably to her mother as they scudded behind a raft of eighteen-wheelers.

Though scared, she would have like to.

Slowly taking her hands off the wheel.

61

They almost ran out of gas. Janis missed three exits; almost as bad, the gas station at the fourth was a self-serve.

Janis pulled into a gas bay and turned off the engine.

Do you know how to do this? Janis said. The butterflies in her stomach had turned to stone, hard grey pebbles, Janis thought, or gravel, weighing her down; things a bird might swallow to aid digestion. Lumps, she thought. A lump: for four and a half months, that was how she had thought of it, despite her increasing belly. She thought she had rid herself of it.

Her mother sat motionless in the car. Do you know anything? Janis wanted to say but stopped herself in time. She got out of the car and saw, to her relief, the instructions on the pump.

She paid with her father's credit card. She also had his CAA membership card in her wallet—just in case, her father had said.

Did you have any trouble? her mother asked when Janis got back into the car.

What kind of trouble did you have in mind?

Half an hour later, just outside St. Catherines, Janis' mother wanted to stop. Back there, she said. Fuck! Janis took both hands off the wheel.

Can you turn around?

Sure. I'll press the Fly Button.

Janis' mother was quiet for several minutes. She scratched her left hand.

Can I smoke in the car then?

Janis' heart lurched. Of course.

Her mother undid her seatbelt. She leaned over and lifted her purse from the floor. I'll put the window down, she said.

You don't have to.

I better. You father can tell.

Eight years after a triple by-pass, Janis' mother still smoked, a fact of which Janis' father remained wholly ignorant, despite the frequently used can of Lysol in the bathroom. Even at the time of the surgery, Janis' mother was unrepentant: she had been allergic to the anaesthetic and languished for ten days in intensive care, thin and jerky when Janis and her father went to visit, a crazed puppet wildly hallucinating; she kept pulling out her IV tubes before the nurses could catch her, hell-bent down the hallway for the smoking lounge.

Her mother never seemed to stop. Still not on solid foods, she called Janis at home one day and asked her to bring two orders of fish and chips—the Chinese ambassador was coming for dinner. And could Janis bring two Cokes? Three days later Janis perched on the ledge outside her mother's window, threatening to jump. Wearing, Janis' mother insisted, a baby bonnet. In the months that followed her mother would be slumped for days and nights in a chair in the living-room, hormones razing every microcell of her newly menopausal body, still achy and seemingly unrecoverable from the hole specialists had made in her chest.

Cigarette butts spilling from an ashtray—years later, driving the car, Janis could still hardly stand to think about it. Occasionally Janis' mother would fall asleep sitting up, cigarette in hand like a glowing watchful eye. Janis, spending half-nights taking in her jeans two inches at least along the inner seam, patching them, would stop on her way to the fridge for a Sprite, slide the cigarette from her mother's fingers and put it out. Her mother hadn't dressed for days—weeks, even, it seemed to Janis, mutely slinking from kitchen to bathroom to bedroom.

Janis' father called from Edmonton. He called from Victoria. He seemed largely unencumbered, unlike Janis' mother grown heavy and loose in her skin as if enamoured of gravity, as if her body bitten back and bifurcated in a forcible entry of nature, rendering her a woman cruelly infarcted, her uterine heart inflected by gravity, with only gravity's nonsense sweet on her tongue. To Janis, her mother's odd clicks and moans, her grappling fingers a code Janis couldn't crack.

Except for an unannounced fear, the look of her mother suddenly old and drooly, unsmiling into sleep. One cigarette. Two.

For weeks Janis came and went in that house—though not really, she never really went. When she lifted a Jonathan Livingston Seagull T-shirt from Big Steel man at Fairview Mall—she had skipped her double French class after lunch to do this—and wore it every day, empty (utterly empty) of intention, what could her mother do? alone in the living-room, alone. Except to shout, You little bitch, you're not my daughter anymore.

As if Janis' body a steel door slamming shut in her mother's face.

What else could her mother do? Her sweet seedlings lost to scorched earth. Her babies finally gone.

She could threaten Janis with a broom at the bottom of the stairs until only Janis' opposite and equal threat caused her mother to stop and take to bed, the house dingy as a cave and oddly carious, with Janis' mother gone so far inside Janis finally gave up calling, asking her mother if she wanted dinner: the frozen peas and carrots, the fried steaks and boiled potatoes Janis in her vague bewilderment made, silently moving about the small kitchen. (Her mother had not eaten for days—weeks, even, it seemed to Janis.)

In the end, Janis left, taking a sleeping-bag to various friends' houses, gone for weeks at a time. For years Janis and her mother were lost to each other in this way.

For the life of her Janis couldn't remember how she and her mother made up with each other. She only knew they must have, dimly, cautiously, because here they were now, together, in the car.

Janis' mother opened her purse and extracted a pack of Belmont Milds. She fumbled at the door, trying to open the car window. Janis, she said. Which button do I press?

Janis stopped at the next Tim Horton's. When they got

back into the car Janis' mother rubbed her hands together vigorously. Okay? she asked. Okie-doke?

We're like two children, Janis thought. Or one child-beast, 24 going on 50 on 10, with two heads like the Pushmi-Pullyo in the Doctor Dolittle book her mother used to read when Janis was five.

Janis smiled. All right, she said. Okay. She put the key in the ignition.

Let's go! her mother said.

Years later Janis thinks she can't remember it all.

Up here on the third floor residents pad around in slippers and housecoats. Visitors bring fresh fruit and candied ginger, the damp smell of winter boots and coats.

Janis' mother sitting in a chair claps her hands in delight; and St. John, New Brunswick—its farmers in gumboots asking her to dance, her! in a pink satin sheath and white satin pumps, frosted pink and pearlized white plastic chips (by the dozen) on earrings that dangle, Chanel No. 15, everything she is able to remember—St. John and its uncouth ignorant men fall away.

Janis marvels at how far her mother has come, from the Maritimes to Montreal to Toronto: a woman who weathered triple bypass at 42 only to lose her mind at 60. Janis and her father decided on the nursing-home after Janis' mother broke her hip last fall, her alarmingly frequent wanderings halted only by a post-menopausal paucity of bone—her mother porous, filled with air and gone, Janis thinks, gone as far as sky. Janis can never catch her now.

Hello there. How's the hip?

Janis brings Cranberry Cove tea and sugarless Kisses, a can of Vernor's, which she and her mother split.

There. Your hair looks better like that. Drink your tea I have to go soon. Put your sweater on, it's cold. Give me your mug. Please extinguish your last cigarette.

Mother, Janis thinks: I bear you no harm.

Janis takes her mother's mostly empty mug to the kitchenette down the hall, the fraught patter of other sons and daughters—all for the sake of the nurses, Janis thinks—provoking in her a chipping, a fury of white chinaware. Such a big show. She feels she is above it all; after all, the parents merely dim now, indifferent as Canadian Shield seen from the window seat of a plane. She thinks of bedrock sheeting entire provinces, nursing-homes like fungal growths proliferating as North America ages.

She swishes hot water in the mug. Swish. Done. She puts it on the Mac-Tacked shelf. Waits, not really wanting to go back to her mother's room.

She should have had a plan. In and out, escaping with her life. And her mother's? Stuck, stuffed thoughtlessly and forever in a dress too young, too old, too flashy: Janis I *need* something; I have nothing to wear, help me pick something—though her closet at home crammed with herringbone, silk, pure new wool barely worn.

Too many choices.

Even so, Janis can finally see what's coming next, end of the road, *obligato* heard on a car radio, one station seeping imperceptibly into the next as the same tune plys all the airwaves, her mother's slow alto push and scrawl counterpointing Janis' own ruthlessly spare and wordless manoeuvrings.

Janis. What should I wear?

As if a change of outfit could change a thing.

Janis knows she will go through her mother's accumulations, excavating the layers garment bag by garment bag, some 30, almost 40, years old. Dresses like froth tossed by waves, wind lifting the gossamer wings of flagrant creatures. Janis will toss and keep and Goodwill will benefit mightily; at least there is comfort in that. Janis will stand before her mother's closet and what will she wear? (Now that her mother can't even dress herself let alone Janis. Now that Janis no longer plays dress-up.) The fifties are back in style. Or was that last year? The seventies are back—but Janis' mother was already old by then. In the high nineties Janis will stand in the body her mother gave her and think, *two thousand*: in two thousand years my mother will be gone.

This is it, Janis thinks, walking back along the hallway to her mother's room: the wide view.

Janis comes, she knows, by her prefigurations honestly, as she too swings low—this small inherited sadness in the dark months since November, the broody months in the steadily darkening years—all the way into her body, so like her mother's, an apple: round at the belly, genetically predisposed to heart attack and stroke and diabetes. Ways in which they let themselves, let everything, go. Janis and her mother still share a sweet, a dangerously sweet, tooth—the dark cravings tiding them through the raving months of winter, a series of days to be somehow gotten through despite a soughing from the belly, this ache, no baby.

No escaping; only forgetting.

Though mostly what Janis misses are her mother's brave pinks and jaunty yellows. Sure signs of spring.

Janis, it's Janis, Mother.

Janis?

Janis sits down on the edge of her mother's bed, then leans over to the night-table. She picks up the phone and calls her father. Five rings, then the answering machine she bought him for Christmas comes on.

Soon there will be no-one to love me, Janis thinks, long and hard, into the noonday sun; though she is often thankful for not having to share her thoughts with anyone. Outside it is almost spring, warmish and watery-bright, though the sidewalks along Bathurst Street are still filthy with winter. She waits for the Lawrence Avenue bus as she waits for spring to arrive, a burst of colour—of fire-engine, Toronto-Transit red—through the gusting greys of March.

Her morning classes are going well; she's a popular lecturer. Afternoons she works on her latest fatuous paper: "Patterns of Discourse in Trollope and Sterne." She works hard, though there are days when everything is a technical difficulty, days when she can't write a word, her putative skills notwithstanding. She waits for the MLA to publish her. She waits for tenure. She waits for her mother to die, to die; awaits death's hot flurry of grief, the dark covering wings Janis thinks beat sometimes against her eyelids.

Tomorrow she will forget where she put her keys and worry for days. Slippage. The short or long skid marks off the road. Life, Janis thinks, at the Thrill-O-Rama: she has become the tightrope walker who briefly disengages to startle the audience in the back row, the special someone who might wave back (though not her mother—not anymore).

She's suddenly acutely tired. She could almost, she thinks, fall asleep right here, here—buses and cars and trucks blasting the asphalt-grey earth, the begrimed March earth at the end of the world, blasting that world to cinders—and go no further. She could almost stop.

Janis' father's not home; she has let herself in with the spare key he still hides in the garage. There, at the back of her mother's closet, Janis finds it. The pink dress rustles against her shoulder. Chanel No. 5 warms her face, as if smoking from the floor beneath her feet—god, it all comes back: her mother's pandemonium body, the terraced grooves and slants, the great swoops and curls of hipbone to thighbone to anklebone. The hushabye hushabye baby.

Pink stuff falls into Janis' eyes.

Janis walk. Janis fall. Into her mother's waiting arms though a woman in heels could easily break a leg carrying a small and squalling child.

Earrings brush Janis' nose. She wants to open her mouth, taste them, until she remembers her mother's stinging slaps to prevent 2 AM trips to Emergency, X-rays, a child's heady foibles amidst the breakneck allure of the world.

Baby come to Mother walking falling.

Janis does, she remembers: her mother carries her in a Godzilla mazurka of feckless grace, her mother does her best, and Tonawanda flames forever behind them.

Here it is, Mother, Janis thinks, standing in front of the closet: the whole wide world.

Janis wonders if her mother would be very much surprised to know her only daughter drinks almost every day now; drives slowly, if at all. At 38 Janis finds she is most like her grampie. He drank himself giddy once—up from New Brunswick for a visit shortly before he died—while the dark of a summer night grew all around him, swathed first his feet, then his legs, then his hands. He sang *Bye baby bunting* while Janis sat by the cedar hedge and waited for her mother and father to come home from a party, a swirl, a lapping, a slapdash of colour through the twilight, almost everything else reduced to light and dark, as in an old photo; her mother, Janis thinks, might have worn cerise, perhaps an ice-cream orange, organdie; though cool ivory would have been the perfect choice on such a hot night.

Janis knows she can't really remember. She'll have to take her mother's word for it.

Boris

Boris walks at night through our house. His face is green, sometimes emerald-green like a lizard's, but only when he's very hungry. I say, Don't go into the basement, and when my brother says, Why? I say, Just don't. My brother cries a little and my mother gets mad: *Big baby*. Then she says, You're scaring your brother. *Miss Smarty-pants*.

When Boris walks up the stairs he keeps his eyes shut tight, not because he's asleep—because he's dead.

The hallway's dark.

My brother and I sit tight, and the light from the TV scrapes our faces blue. The mad doctor laughs, and I try not to spill from the tray on my lap as I pass my brother his drink. When the doctor laughs again my brother and I press our heads to the back of the couch.

There's a boy who plays at the edge of the woods. All by himself. A crowd gathers in town. They shout, wave torches. I'm letting my brother eat Cheerios and he sucks each mouthful to a soft whine, and his pyjamas crisp nice against my shoulder.

The air crackles and pops, blue and white explosions.

The boy looks up. Stumbles, faints.

When something drags him deep into the woods the doctor laughs and laughs and I hold the tray tight as men and women scream, mouths cracked into Os of surprise.

I stop chewing, mouth full of crumble.

Listen, I tell my brother, and I nod toward the hallway. It's Boris. Can't you hear him?

The TV spits fire, spits lightning and I can see my brother's face—how he just *looks*.

I lean closer.

March march march, I say, and I tell him how my ears pound against my head.

I told my brother something. Last Saturday afternoon in the parking-lot at the grocery store. My mother parked the car. Got out, then leaned back inside. She looked me hard in the eye.

When a strange man knocks on the door don't let him in. Don't let your brother out.

She left and I rolled the car windows up tight. I locked the doors shut. I counted *wait-wait*, tick-tock like a clock. Then I said, sharp as scissors, Don't move.

He kicked the seat in front of him, testing. We'd played this before: the steering-wheel a throat, the dashboard alive with tortures.

I clicked and growled.

I said, Believe me.

Air still as cliffs, like waiting for something to start or to stop—slip over the waiting, fall all the way forward.

Then there's only my brother, sitting still in the car like he's frozen. Outside the car window, people push grocery carts, pineapples stiff through the tops of bags. People unlock their trunks, their doors, they get in their cars and go home. But I'm still saying, It'll get you—I don't stop.

And after a while I do.

Then my brother and I wait quietly in the car for my mother, but it seems like forever. And in the summer forever's very hot. In the winter it's very cold.

I think Boris' heart is like that, misery thickened to heavy machinery and it turns and turns and inside its cold parts (somewhere *in there*) I can hear my own voice.

The TV gurgles now, it hisses. Boris walks.

After the first movie. After the crackers and toast. After the first half of the second movie, when my brother falls asleep, and I wake him.

Bed, I say.

I take him down the hallway to his room. I put the covers

over him and he's so sleepy, tomorrow he won't remember how he got there.

From the hallway I can see the TV flash and fade, and I don't look down the stairs. When I go back into the room and turn off the TV it smokes to grey then dies to black.

I lie in my bed.

All night long, Boris.

His arms stretch in front of him and his hands open and shut, open and shut, very slowly, and they're white with wormy grey veins, and his hands are very strong, and cold. When I pee the bed it's hot and the hotness makes my legs warm.

But then the pee grows cold, and smells bad, and I know my mother will yell in the morning.

You could never stop him. This is something I know, and I don't know if my brother knows it, but I do, and that's all that matters.

So I never even try.

What my brother and I know for sure is this: there are bad people. We're not so sure about good people.

Bela.

My brother and I hold hands above the vampire. Close our eyes.

Bel-ah.

Chase each other over the bed, under the bed. Tear around the wastepaper basket until I bang into it—blue, green, yellow construction paper spews out, and we trample it and yell at each other, we yell at the top of our lungs—I vant to suck your blood—until our mother shouts up the stairs.

You kids'll be the death of me.

Bela's cape looks like my father's best tweed jacket. My brother picked the cape up before the paint dried, fingerprints on the black outside and on the red inside. Okay. Bela's an *English* vampire who roams the moors by night. Very polite when he greets his guests at Buckingham.

Good eve-eh-ning.

Step right this way, over here we have the famous Creature, the Creature from the Black Lagoon. The hardest to put together. First we lost his spiny tail. A star of claws went next. We take him out of the box and lie him on the floor and small bits of plastic surround him like a magic circle. Kick some away, by accident, and they're like a trail of crumbs, and we can follow them to the Creature's wandering tail.

My brother says, When.

Supper's ready. You kids get down here now.

Boris. Nothing's missing. His skin shines dull as a dead man's. Pants tattered, black like the black knobs on each side of his head. Only I can place him back in his box to rest, wrapped in green tissue paper and bits of silver tinsel left over last Christmas.

Handle with care! Disease! Injury!

My brother's still wondering about the Creature.

It's fun knowing more than someone else.

She'll have to go upstairs and clean up after us. She knows it. Fishsticks. Coke and canned peaches. She says she's the Shit-Lady, and all we ever do is shit on her. That's all people'll ever do to you. You and your so-called friends. (Listen to the mouth on her, my father says.)

After supper my brother and I go outside. We split a Vachon cake. In the morning dragonflies ride double in the ditch and the grass flattens damp under your feet. But at seven o'clock the trees darken to fists and the birds cry loud and long and you can look for them as long as you like and never see one at all.

We turn the corner from Hillcrest Crescent onto Princess Street. It's almost summer-warm. The fall leaves rot sweet into my nose.

That's where Wendy fell off her bike when the chain grabbed her foot and she tried to turn the handlebars but the gravel jerked her tires. Off she went—ten feet at least straight through the air and into the ditch, and her skirt flew around her head. (When I told my father, he wanted to know, Could you see her bare arse? Yes, you could, I said. You could see her bare arse.)

And yesterday I went looking, and I found a yellow streamer from Wendy's handlebars, wrapped tight around a rock in the ditch, but I never gave it back.

Underwear, the bare tops of Wendy's legs. Arse.

I didn't used to know how to ride a bike. My cousin Ruth showed me. We were at her house by the lake. Uncle Roy fell asleep on the floor, after my father took my mother and Ruth's mother shopping. Uncle Roy drinks. Like candy to a baby, my mother says. My father says, Imagine, a grown man. My mother says, What do you expect. Mumma spoiled him.

Ruth and I went outside. We had purple liquorice strings to tie together or braid, and foamy powder kegs that fizz up your nose when you suck the liquorice wick. She took me behind her house (Shack, my father calls it) and I found a frog. Ruth said, No, it's a toad.

The lake shone blue. My nose hurt.

Ruth said, Come over here. Hurry. But there were nails everywhere (junk, junk heap) so I had to go slow. Big boards, rusted metal growing up like grass.

She stood beside the tool shed, holding two corners of a big dirty sheet, as high as my waist, higher, lumpy, orange-brown. Dirty water and dead bugs caught in its folds.

Abra-cadabra.

A hush like wings flapping. And then from the house a door slammed, and my cousin Ruth had that big orange sheet only half-way up. Breeze catching at the edges—and I froze, too.

My father calling to me. He must have left our mothers in town. They drive him crazy, two old broads.

We could hear him, kicking the garbage can by the steps. Calling me. Saying, little bitch, when I didn't answer.

74

I looked at Ruth. Pull it off, I thought. Pull it. And when my father called again I thought, Don't.

A door slammed a second time, and the house was quiet. She pulled off the cover. Her new bike shone blue, like it'd been skimmed off the top of the lake. We didn't say anything for a moment.

Nice bike.

She said, Ride it!

So I did, straight down the path behind the house and into the woods, and the lake flashed like coins through slots of trees, silver, silver-blue, silver and the blue of the bike high above the lake.

I rode that bike fast—and what Ruthie told everybody later was wrong, I rode it really far, then I stopped. And lying between rocks and roots on the path, I could see the blood on my knee was even brighter than Ruthie's bike.

My brother and I check the ditch on Princess Street again. Nothing there, so we climb back out. I can see Wendy and her older sister Marie, but they're far off, at least half-way up the street and close to Willowdale Avenue where the cars all go.

Wendy and Marie are talking to Kathy Martin, who's taller than Marie, taller than even the boys in the Grade 5 class at school. Their shorts dust to grey in the twilight. I want to catch up, but the stones from the side of Princess Street catch in the backs of my flip-flops, and each time I stop to shake the stones out my brother says, Rather we go home.

Four-year-old in blue seersucker pyjamas and a straw tourist-hat from Mexico, fringed with red pom-poms. *Rather* he do this, *Rather* that.

Know-it-all, my mother says to me sometimes. My brother's face a tight hard rock that won't budge. His big words make me angry because now it's him, not me, who thinks he knows.

His cake's gone, but I still have the wrapper to lick clean.

We have to go up the street.

I wave my tongue across the plastic in slow hard circles like I'm waving a wand, and the caramel tastes so good.

He's looking at the wrapper. Too afraid to turn back without me.

The streetlights are still off. I want to see them come on, all at once but all I see are the twirly bats as they fall through the near-dark around us.

When I get to 224 Princess Street I stop. He's ten steps behind me so I turn around and wait. Dark-green curtains in the window, full of shadow. Wrought-iron railing up the dark-brown steps. Cracked. Steep. Even the untrimmed shrubs that line the long drive.

He catches up.

Look.

But he can't, he's so scared he runs and it's funny, how his arms and legs jerk in different directions at once like they might snap right off.

I pass the house. Curtains move.

(I'm sure.)

Run.

In Kathy Martin's kitchen the spoons go somewhere else.

I hold one in my hand and reach up and pull open the white drawer, but only half-way. Kathy Martin laughs and says, It always sticks. Reaches down and pulls it open for me.

Wendy and her older sister Marie wipe the pots and pans.

Nobody turns the kitchen light on so the streetlight from Willowdale Avenue shines in the window. Kathy Martin opens the fridge door. That light shines too.

I think I hear a bus go by. Not sure, so I don't say.

When I look inside the drawer I look hard at the tray but I can only see forks where my mother would put the spoons. I can see plastic corn cobs at the bottom of the tray, and I don't even know what they're for.

76

My brother sits in a chair in the corner. I can't see him too well. He has his hat on, and he's quiet. Looking around, swinging his legs.

Nobody tells him to stop.

I look harder at the tray. She could take the spoon-drying away from me.

I look down at my hand—pretty spoon, so smooth, and warming, now, against my palm. Red handle, metal joints with bits of food caked in them. What the washing missed. Crusted with pinky cream, and the smooth round inside still streaked from when somebody sucked their last spoonful, too full to eat another mouthful. Full to the brim.

My brother's laughing. Kathy gives him a popsicle. But to Wendy and Marie and me she only gives tall glasses of water.

Then Kathy Martin says, Spoons over there, and points to the left of the knives.

I drop my spoon in, dry two more.

When Kathy Martin's father comes into the kitchen he turns the light on. He looks like my father asleep, face twisted swollen like a balloon the day after it's pumped up. Air shrinking inside.

At first Kathy Martin's father just looks at us. He's been sleeping. His chest is hairy and his underwear bags loose around his legs. He bangs his fist down on the counter and the still-dirty dishes bounce up and clink. Rubs his hands over his face. Walks over to the table and pulls out a chair, slowly tilts it back. He makes a noise and I think he's saying something, but Kathy Martin and Marie hold onto their glasses and don't say a word, so I can't really tell.

Oh.

My brother's popsicle melts cherry-red down his arm. Sticky. He doesn't notice.

I'm not going to clean it up, I don't care.

Wendy starts to hiccough, she always does when she's

scared—she can't stop. I think, Shut up. Please. Then Kathy Martin's father says, Jesus, very slowly. Jee-sus. And he lets the chair fall.

Fuckers, he says. Get the fuck home.

Boris, lips seepy-fat blisters.

Listen, I tell my brother. Listen. He does.

My brother and I yelling, hot with hot laughs, dizzy.

And once, my mother came into my room late at night. This is something I never tell.

Wake up. We're leaving.

She dressed me, but she forgot one sock, and I liked how my bare foot felt inside my boot—strange. Like someone else's foot.

My heel rubbing against the felt liner.

We walked to the park on Spring Garden Avenue. She talked fast. Words I couldn't put together, and by themselves they didn't make sense.

Brown gloved hand on my arm. She brushed my hair out of my eyes.

The lights from the houses on the street above the park looked warm. She was laughing. Saying things like, Oh, and the time, then laughing before she finished talking and holding my hand and jerking it when she got excited.

Then she laughed and rode the slide, even though it was wet with snow. I watched to make sure she didn't slip backward and bump her head, the way she sometimes did for my brother and I. After the slide she wanted to ride the teeter-totter, so I sat on the opposite end from her and she laughed as she jerked me into the air.

At first I laughed, too. And then I didn't—riding high-up and the houses on the street above us silent and frozen.

And I held on tight because I thought I might fall, squeezed hard against the giant arc of rusted metal creaking like a breath held up or down on the in or out, all that still cold air turning inside me.

My eyes watered hard against the sharp night—I knew there was no-one to catch me. Until up that high all I could see were the black spaces between the up and down swing of blue and red metal, the houses just blurs of light.

A blurry star moving at the top of the hill.

My mother stopped.

We walked up the hill and got into the car. My father drove us home. She was quiet. He said, Don't tell your friends about your crazy mother.

I'm eight. I'm ten. I'm twelve.

Sometimes I don't think about much, being older, and the old games so stupid. I go out with my friends. My brother stays in his room and adds this to that with his chemistry set. Test tubes foam, surge with secret formulas. Break. Guess he doesn't know much, like how to put the parts together.

Snap, snap crackle pop.

And sometimes. Boris only a dream at night, foggy, a man in my room. Sitting in a chair. Go back to sleep, he says. He moves his hands over my legs, is it cold. Can I run. Maybe it's hot.

My father always says, Go back to sleep.

And there was that time once, at the end of Princess Street, before you turn onto Hillcrest Crescent and walk the three doors to our house, when I stopped running and turned around.

I can see him up the road, moving through the dark between the streetlights toward me. He's lost his Mexican hat, and as he gets closer I can see his mouth snap open and shut, open and shut. Very fast.

I can't hear a thing.

Or I hear something, like something's spinning or chug-chugging only it's not my brother and it's not me, or is it.

And coming up to me like that on Princess Street his face looked funny. All surprised and jangly, like he was all beaten up inside. He was crying, and I hit him and hit him, we were so afraid, and I was so mad.

And that's what it was like, being young and having a little brother—just no good people, maybe. And a Creamsicle, or maybe a chocolate float.

You eat it fast. You try not to make a mess.

LISA MOORE

The Nipple of Paradise

I expected some epiphany during the birth. Some way to order the material, some profound wisdom. It seems important to document exactly the way it went. In fact I would like to set the whole summer down in point form. Collect it, pin it. The birth, the affair, the post-partum-affair depression. Already I remember the summer in shorthand, distilled. It's made up of only a hundred or so specific images all intermingled; meals, sex, nights on the fire excape, hours in the office, the birth, the affair. And by next summer I won't even remember it that clearly. But for now it has reached the half-dissolved stage, the separate gestures of the summer exaggerated like the colour in polaroids.

After I found out that Cy slept with Marie I sat on the fire escape with my foot on the banister, and a spider crawled over my foot, my toes tensed and each toe stretching away from the others, I could feel the spider make its web, lacing my toes together. It struck me that I had never felt anything so sharply before. That's how I think a story should work. Like that Chinese ribbon dance. They turn off the lights so you can't see the dancer. All you see are two long fluorescent ribbons drawing in the dark. That's like the strokes of the summer. Or that guy Volker we met in Germany who was an artist, did drawings with a pen flashlight inside a cave and a photographer he knew shot them with fast speed film. Volker was a shadow but he drew the outline of men and women embracing. He said it took incredible concentration because you only had ten seconds to make the drawing. The result was a fury of limbs licked through each other, the lines themselves seared onto the walls of a cave, the condensation glittering like sweat. That's how I would like this story to work, to blink the summer at you, see if there's any epiphany.

Example: Hannah, Cy's daughter, in her satin ballet costume, black with red sequins, lime green tulle, dragging herself up the staircase, howling like a wolf, "I got no-one to play with. I got no-one to play with," hand over hand on the banister while the sky blisters with rain, while Cy and I make love in the bathroom. He's soaking in this chemical blue bubblebath Hannah bought him for Christmas the first year I met him. It comes out of a plastic bottle shaped like a Havana nightclub dancer. The woman's hat, a mountain of bananas, unscrews, and although the bubbles are turquoise the bath-room stinks of synthetic bananas. We try to make love first on the side of the tub but it's slippery from the steam, then on the toilet, and then one foot on the radiator, hiked up on the sink so I can see my own sunburnt face in the antique mirror we found in an abandoned house around the bay. The mirror is watery, my face wobbles with laughter because the position is so ridiculous, my legs bound by the pink maternity overalls wrapped around my knees and Hannah banging now on the bathroom door. Cy comes, and then both of us completely still, him hugging me from behind we look at each other's faces in the mirror. His hand is on my belly and the baby kicks so hard both our eyes widen at the same time. We answer Hannah in unison, "Just a second." I haul up my overalls while Cy opens the door. "Jeez," says Hannah and sits on the toilet to pee.

After the baby was born and I was still drugged, I thought I felt her move again, inside me. I guess it's like when they say someone feels an itch in a missing limb. It was only a ghost of the way she felt inside me, and already I was forgetting what it felt like to have her flutter in there. Like a million years had passed.

I didn't really get the chance to read very much birthing literature. I'd collected it, seen a film of an Australian woman who gave birth in her own living-room. The next door neigh-bour dropped over, made himself a cup of tea and ended up holding the mirror for her, between her legs. She wore an old T-shirt and moaned in an Australian accent. The baby was blue when it came out. Cy gritted his teeth while he watched.

Our Bodies Our Selves says that some male partners seek other sexual partners during the pregnancy. "You wouldn't do that, would you Cy?"

We only got to one of the pre-natal classes. It happened to be the one on "Things that can go wrong." The nurse started off by assuring everyone that in most cases nothing goes wrong but we had to go through this anyhow, just in case. She showed the suction cups the doctors sometimes use during natural births. They had pink cups and blue cups, the nurse told us, "... but as sure as shooting if you used the pink cup you'd get a boy and vice versa. Now the funny thing about these cups is they seem to go in and out of fashion, like you might notice a certain doctor using them for a couple of months and then it seems like they stay in the cupboard for six months and nobody uses them. They don't hurt the baby, of course, except they do sometimes come out with cone-shaped heads when the doctor uses the suction cups. In fact you have to be careful after you have the baby that you lay him on different sides every time you lay him down, otherwise his head will go flat. Actually, there's a little community up the southern shore that's into head sculpting, all of them got heads as flat as frying-pans on one side." And she snorted, "No, that's only a joke."

She said the last time she brought the forceps to a lecture one of the dads got real upset, so this time she was only bringing a diagram. She held up the diagram for a moment without comment and then slid it behind the next diagram, which was of a baby whose head was too big to fit through the pelvic hole. At the end of the session she got everyone to lie down on a mat and she played a relaxing tape. "Come on now dads, don't be shy, down on the mats with the moms." She turned the lights off so the room was black. Cy and I lay down on a gym mat and listened while a sultry female voice told us our toes, ankles, knees, hipjoints and so on up the body were feeling feather-light, as if all the tension of the day was leaving our bodies in waves. There was a soundtrack of waves and sitar music in the background. Beside me I could feel Cy's shoulder shuddering in a silent fit of giggles.

I guess I should describe Marie. She was beautiful and unemployed all summer. Thick curly black hair, long sun-tanned legs. She didn't believe in marriage. Not only did she never plan to marry but she didn't acknowledge anyone else's marriage. She said she has a Marxist approach to the whole thing. "Love isn't a commodity. A wife is a whore, only real whores are more honest about it and have more fun. Marriage is a business contract whereby women sell men exclusive sex rights, accessing the male to control over the means of repro-duction in exchange for financial security. Romantic love is a corrupt notion that leads ultimately to death by excruciating boredom. Besides, I can't help how I feel about Cy." And she winked at me.

Marie, the night I found out they slept together: Cy has invited her to supper. She brings us chocolates wrapped in gold foil with miniature Rembrandt paintings. Rembrandt's fat creamy wife. Cy is excited about the wrappers because he's working on a thesis for an Art History degree. He collects everybody's wrapper and begs Marie to eat the last chocolate. She laughs and tosses it at his chest. It bounces off and nearly hits the baby rocking in her daycradle beside Cy's chair.

The Party: we are having fondue. Cy spilled the starter fluid and when he lights it the whole thing bursts into flames. The table is full of flammable things we somehow hadn't noticed before: dishtowels, the bottle of starter fluid, a yellow styro-foam duck that Hannah's art teacher made for parents who volunteered to wear it on their heads for a swimathon for cancer. Cy and I are screaming at each other. Hannah comes into the kitchen and we both scream, "Get out of the kitchen" in unison. Marie promptly throws a dishtowel on the fondue pot. There are a few clouds of black smoke. She lifts it off, magician-like, and there are no more flames. We stare at the pot for a few seconds and the flames burst back to life. The heat reaches the neck of the duck, melting it, so the duck's beak opens angrily. Marie puts the cloth back on and the fire is out. Later in the evening everybody is drunk and raucous except me, because I'm still pregnant. We have eaten all evening, asparagus, carrots, broccoli dipped in hot wine-cheese fondue, chunks of pumpernickel bread. Someone has suggested I wear the styrofoam duck on my head throughout the evening. I protested but everyone booed me, so rather than seeming excruciatingly boring I wear it. Marie picks up an empty wine bottle and blows into it. It sounds eerie and hollow and for a minute it sobers everyone. Suddenly Marie's chair collapses beneath her. In slow motion she reaches both her arms out to Cy, their fingers grip for a second and she hits the floor. She is laughing so hard she's in tears.

The Birth: she came a month-and-a-half early. A thirty-weeker, as they call them in the neo-natal nursery. It was a caesarean. We arrived at the hospital at one in the morning and entered the case room. The nurses' station glowed like a space ship because the lights in the hall were dimmed. The nurse looked at me with a raised eyebrow as if my street clothes were a faux-pas. They took Cy and me to a room and smeared jelly over my belly and hooked me to monitors. The baby's heart rate was scratched out on a spewing paper in fine red ink. The doctor came and said I should be operated on right away. He had two caesareans ahead of me.

"Each of them will take a half-hour or so and then we'll do you," and that must have been exactly how long they took because they were back in an hour. In the delivery-room, everyone was masked and wearing paper hats covered with mauve and blue flowers. A giant convex mirror hung from the ceiling but I had to be hunched up in a fetal position. The epidural was like freezing water dribbling down my spine. They put a blue curtain across my chest and gathered around the table, which was uncomfortably narrow. The anaesthetist was at my head. He sat next to a large box with dials and monitors. There was still a tube in my back in case something went wrong and he had to administer more anaesthetic. Somebody was shaving my pubic hair.

"How's that?"

"He likes it lower than that."

"Where's Cy?" I asked.

"We'll let Cy in when we're ready," the anaesthetist said.

When Cy came in he was wearing a mauve and pink flowered cap also. He kneeled next to me, holding my hand, smoothing my hair. "I can still feel my toes," I said.

"It's not your toes we're operating on," said the anesthetist. "You will feel sensation, you'll feel them cutting you, but no pain."

I heard them pull the tray of instruments across the floor. Suddenly I was swept with fear and just as suddenly it was gone. I felt the knife pressing across my belly. Cy began to smooth my hair with more vigour until his stroke became so vigorous I had to stop him. There was a sucking noise.

"That was your water breaking," said someone behind the curtain. The anaesthetist looked over the curtain.

"Black hair," he said, "It's a girl."

"Is she healthy?" I asked.

"Appears to be."

The sense of relief was absolute. As soon as I found out I was pregnant I planned to write about the birth. I figured the epiphany would come then, that I would be wiser, at that moment, the moment of birth. But I was dumbfounded, it struck me walking down the street yesterday. For the ten days I was in hospital I didn't write a word. Not a letter or thank-you note. It took us a month and a half to figure out a name for her. I couldn't find any significance, the birth wasn't a symbol or metaphor, it just happened, a clean thing, a thing unto itself, a pure wordless thing. I think I was struck dumb.

They laid her on my chest. Her head was small as a fist. Green guck of some sort all over her hair. The anaesthetist put his hand over her closed eyes to block the light so she would open them. They were black and wet like those of a newborn kitten. We held her there while they sewed me up. Cy said he saw her in the mirror first, being passed from hand to hand. Then all the doctors shook Cy's hand, congratulating him.

The nurses in the neo-natal said Cy was the best father they'd seen. They said, "She'll have him wrapped around her little finger."

There were four other women besides me at the breastfeeding class they offer in the hospital. We all had self-righteous expressions, we had heard that only 30% of Newfoundland women breastfeed. The nurse speaks without stopping for breath, "Now girls some of the dads might be uncomfortable with the breastfeeding at first but sure that's only natural. You'll find that when you climax while you're having sex you'll probably be squirting milk all over him, just keep a towel handy that's all, and don't worry about the public, nobody cares unless you're in the mall and you strip off down to the waist, now you know yourself girls you have to use a little common sense and girls, if you're going to a cocktail party, double pad girls because I'm telling you now once you get a drop of wine in you it's going to be like Churchill Falls and you're going to have to go in the bathroom and wring out your cocktail dress."

The nurse puts on an instructional video in which a 50-year-old woman holds a stuffed doll to her blouse in the various different breastfeeding positions. She holds it under one arm, the legs kicking behind and white letters appear on the screen. "Football position." Then the video shows actual mothers who look worn out, still in hospital johnny coats, close-ups on their breasts, which are swollen, blue-veined and mountainous next to the newborn babies. Breastfeeding is a skill, the narrator tells us.

My baby was too small to suck from my nipple so we had to feed her pumped breast milk from a bottle. I had to pump every night. Fit the plastic cone over my swollen rock-hard breast and flick the little lever that starts the pump. I've seen the pump that we use to get water from the well. This pump was the same size. A $2000 machine. It makes a loud grinding noise. After three days I thought I was bonding with it. Cy sat with me while my milk squirted into the attached cup. I showed him the four-ounce mark "Look how much I got."

"That's great Donna."

In the long exhausted week after she was born we went to the area off the cafeteria so Cy could smoke. It's a small room with a few tables, tinfoil ashtrays, lit mostly by the lights in the snack machines. A lattice of stained wood, shaped like an arch, separated the area from the rest of the cafeteria but it was as if this decorating effort was only half-hearted because the garden motif ended there. There were meals of macaroni and soup that could be heated in the microwave, all displayed in racks that rotated when you pushed a button. At ten at night we had the area off the cafeteria to ourselves except for a nurse who came in with a flattened piece of shiny paper. She put it in the microwave and watched it like a TV, pulling over a rickety chair and resting her elbows on her knees, chin in hand. The microwave choked into action, the inside lit up and a red light played on the package until it expanded with bursting popcorn kernels into a round smooth ball that split in a line up the centre. When she left Cy reached into the pocket of his coat and pulled out a small box.

"I got you something."

It was a bottle of moisturizing cream. I had run out but I told Cy not to get any because we couldn't afford it. This made tears come to my eyes.

Cy said, "Ah, for Jesus sake Donna."

"Well, I'm tired Cy, I'm just plain tired."

I guess it was somewhere during that week he slept with Marie. I found out because of the baby monitor. We got this monitor, you put one piece in the baby's cradle and the other you carry around with you. It's so sensitive you can hear the baby breathe or hiccough. It took a little getting used to, sometimes it would pick up the voices of children playing on

the street, the sound would be garbled and static as if the baby
had been invaded by aliens who were using her as a vehicle to
speak their message. Once at midnight Cy and I were sitting
at the living-room table having a cup of coffee, watching the
couples coming up from the Ship Inn, when there was a loud
crash over the monitor. Both of us froze for a second and then
ran up the stairs, taking them two at a time. In her room everything was still. The bassinet was in the centre of the table
where we had left it. Cy looked out the window—somebody
on the street had slammed a car door.

The night Marie came over for supper Cy took her up to the
bedroom to see the baby. He forgot the monitor was on. He
said, "Listen Marie, what happened, if Donna knew about it,
it would really hurt her, I mean I really had a good time, but I
think it was a sort of solitary thing."

His voice was soft and without static, it was almost as if he
were standing behind me, telling me about it. I went out on
the fire escape with my cup of coffee, put my feet up on the
banister and cried.

I had been so weak the whole time I was in hospital. The
baby was the smallest baby in the neo-natal nursery. I was okay
when Cy was with me, but when I had to go into the nursery
by myself I was convinced they were going to tell me something terrible. They have huge stainless-steel sinks with digital clocks that tell you how many seconds you've been scrub-
bing. While I washed up to the elbow I would have to
convince myself not to start crying. Once I went in and they
said, "Now Mrs. Sheppard I better tell you this before you see
your baby, there's nothing to worry about but she stopped
breathing for a minute or so. That's common with premature
babies, one of the nurses noticed she was a little dusky-
coloured and picked her up and she was fine. But we got a
monitor on her now and I just wanted to mention it before you
saw her, so you'd know there was nothing to worry about."

I phoned Cy and he said he'd be up right away. I stood in the
bathroom of my hospital-room looking in the mirror,

smoothing the moisturizing cream over my face. When Cy got there he held me in his arms a long time. When visiting hours were over he went home and phoned me. They had wheeled a patient into my room who had just given birth so I couldn't talk, I could only listen.

Cy read to me from a history book about Christopher Columbus. Columbus wrote to Ferdinand that he had sighted cyclops and mermaids, not as beautiful as previously reported, in fact quite mannish. They believed back then that the garden of Paradise was on Earth. That the world was pear-shaped and a protuberance on the top, like a woman's nipple, that was where the garden of Eden was. When Columbus found South America he knew he had come to land because fresh water was mixing with sea water and whales played there. He thought that fresh water flowed from the nipple of paradise. When I woke up the telephone receiver was buzzing the dial tone in my ear.

Out on the fire escape the fog coming up from the harbour penetrated my clothes and a spider crawled over my foot. Cy came out and I said to him, "Cy, how do I know you won't leave me?" He said, "You don't know Donna, all I know is I love you fiercely right now, that's the best I can offer you."

I thought about that artist Volker we visited in Germany. He had taken Cy and me into his painting studio and showed us paintings for two hours. Suddenly, he said, "Come here Cyril, I will show you something." He grabbed Cy's thumb and dipped it into a can of gold pigment, powdered gold. Cy held up his gilded thumb. It looked like a fragment of an ancient statue was somehow attached to his living hand. It made me think of Hansel and Gretel, how the witch said show me your thumb so I can see if you're fattened up and Hansel held out a chicken bone. Buying precious time. It made me think that love is made of isolated flashes and they are what we crave. It was getting dark outside Volker's studio and Cy's thumb glowed like something expensive, timeless.

Haloes

Haloes are the vibration of that which is perfect. Once the fish in the harbour of St. John's were so thick and silver they slowed sailing vessels. The great fire of 1892 razed the city when it became imperfect. Now sometimes, something is added, a hoar frost, a shipment of mangoes, the fog and the equation of the city can't contain its perfection. There's a surplus, you must stand very still to see it. Perfection spills over in a glow at the edges of the city.

There's a photograph of the house my parents built together when it was just a skeleton. Blond two-by-fours like a rib-cage around a lungful of sky. They worked back to back shifts in the restaurant they sold before I was born. The house was built on the weekends. I never once heard my parents make love, or saw them naked together. But the photograph of the two-by-fours is like walking in on them, unexpected. The house without its skin. Their life together raw, still to come.

I sat on the bar stool next to Philip. I can talk to Philip only when I'm drunk. I know things about him. He has a small daughter in Germany. He doesn't talk much. At the bar I said to him, Now Philip how do you justify having a kid in Germany? Some poor young woman taking care of a baby all by herself? Philip barely moves his lips when he talks. There's a lisp like a run in a silk stocking. A ventriloquist throwing his voice into his own mouth.

He has that weird relationship with alcohol few people can maintain. He soaks himself in it every night without ever letting it own him. He's 36 and it hasn't ruined his face. Instead of making him old it's kept him from ever maturing, from ever making enough money to leave the city. He's a drummer. When he's drumming hard it's like another face lives in his face, his true expression. Red and blue lights float over him like tropical fish. There's something sexually magnetic about Philip's drinking, as if he could easily ignite.

His face turned red. I was still giggling. We had been walking across a lake of clear alcohol, our fingertips barely touching, and suddenly lost belief in our buoyancy. I know a woman who left her house at two in the morning and knocked on his door. He was watching television with a remote, the empty walls reflecting a syncopated beating, like butterfly wings. He had a plaid wool blanket wrapped around his knees. Whatever happened between them wasn't pleasant and she didn't want to say anything much about it. She said he had just finished an orange and two of his fingers were sticky, webbed together. She separated his fingers with her tongue, tasting the orange pulp. This is a strange detail, but I have picked up a few esoteric things like this about Philip without even listening for them. He eats Marmite. Once some teenagers lured him into an alley and beat him with pickets torn from a fence, breaking two of his ribs. When he's absolutely drunk he can sink every ball on a pool table. I asked about his daughter again, not making the connection between his red face and his rage.

He didn't raise his voice. He said, If you were a man I'd punch you in the face. What a stupid question. How can you ask something like that. If you don't get away from me I will punch your face in. You're a mother. I can't believe you're a mother. You haven't learned anything in your whole life.

I almost asked Philip to punch me. I willed it. A smash in the face would even things out, tip me off the bar stool. I realized that over ten years I had only gathered little splinters of Philip.

That afternoon I had been on the verandah with my daughter blowing psychedelic bubbles. Someone guessed the bubble solution was saturated with glycerine and that's what made the colour so lurid. Hot pink, chartreuse, turquoise. The bubbles trembled. One even touched the splintery wood rail without breaking. My daughter and I, shadows stretching over the surface, bursting. I slid off the bar stool and went back to my seat before Philip decided to hit me. He stood up and pulled on his bomber jacket. It was a grey nylon, and the wrinkles in his back seemed to shimmer a one-hundred-proof hatred as delicate as a bubble.

That night I dreamed I was about to take a penis in my mouth, but there was a jagged piece of glass embedded in it, and it split my lower lip. Blood gushed freely and I got weak, the same weakness that happens when you give blood. A beatific lightness that absolved me.

This incident with Philip was nothing. Something he probably wouldn't remember in the morning. But it sank inside me. It made me avoid the cafés and stores and streets where I thought I might run into him. It made me want to leave the city. Move away.

I'm reading one of the volumes of the "History of Haiku" that Albert Austin left for me before he committed suicide. He was someone else whose pain I brushed up against accidentally. I knew him only one night, we went on a blind date. He was an American, a draft dodger who had set up a false-eyelash company in Ontario, a front to employ illegal immigrants, he said. He followed a woman to Newfoundland. He took me to an expensive restaurant, but he couldn't taste any of the food. Albert had no sense of smell. He talked fast, I hardly said anything. The restaurant emptied. The waiters were leaning against the back wall waiting to go home. He kept talking. He said he was rich. He was working on sonar radar graphics, writing a program that could draw icebergs three-dimensionally for free-floating oil rigs. You're only seeing the very tip, he said. His heart wasn't in it, though. He was thinking he'd buy a fast convertible, drive to Mexico. I could go if I wanted. He did buy the convertible shortly after our date, I heard. He bought it and left town for a month. Then he came back and left the Haiku books for me in the restaurant where I was working, did a few other errands and drove the silver convertible off Red Cliff. I couldn't understand why he had driven back here from Mexico to commit suicide. He had lived in St. John's for only the last five years of his life.

I read "the haiku is like a finger pointing at the moon. It's important that it's not a bejewelled or perfect finger. It only points to something." I met Mike, my husband, after that. We were out drinking and Mike brought me home to his apartment. It was Albert's old apartment. Mike had used the last of Albert's shaving-cream, wore a pair of Albert's construction boots that were left under the bathroom sink. They fit him perfectly.

My mother-in-law, Louise, is a real-estate agent. The best in St. John's. In the weekend paper there's a whole page, a pyramid of real-estate agents' photographs. Louise is always at the top, or the second line from the top. They're placed according to their sales. Louise is afraid of two things. Fire and cats. She says when she was a baby, a cat lay over her face, filling her mouth and nose with fur, almost suffocating her. She was less than two years old but she remembers it. Cats are attracted to the smell of milk on the baby's breath. She didn't want us to buy this house. A fire trap, she said.

I was sewing a dress for my step-daughter with a friend who lives on the other side of the city. We were drinking coffee and Tia Maria. The phone rang and it was Mike. He said he was standing in the front doorway of our house. The fire was pouring down the street. He said they were safe, but embers as big as his fist were dropping at his feet. The sky is orange, he said. I pulled the phone over to the window. There was an orange and black cloud breathing in the sky on the other side of the city. I said, That's over my house. He said, You should see it, it's like lava in the street. They'll evacuate us when it gets hot enough.

I ran home. Some streets were blocked. Ours was a frozen river from the fire hoses. A blizzard of orange flakes. I had to cover my head with my scarf to keep my hair from catching fire. Mike had closed the front door because of the soot and smoke. The radio said if the fire reached our street the whole of downtown would be lost. It said the firemen were losing control. There were high winds. A policeman rapped on the door with a billy knocker. He said, Move now, NOW. The street was full of people carrying blankets, photo albums, figurines. A spark landed on my daughter's hand, making a tiny burn. We went to my sister's and stayed up all night listening to the radio, drinking, unable to get drunk. At three in the morning the radio said they had contained it. Our house was safe. I felt a quick stab of disappoinment. I wasn't comfortable in the city anymore.

Since the fire the house has become infested with mice. The cat is playing with a mouse now, under my chair. I have my feet drawn up on the seat. I smash the mouse under a book. I smash it three times as hard as I can. When I lift the book off, the mouse is flattened. But then it pops back, like a mouse in a pop-up storybook. The cat finally bites its head. I hear the crunching of the bones of its skull between the cat's teeth; althought the body is still moving, the tail has become a stiff S. In a few seconds the cat has devoured the entire body. She gives a cry. I half expect the mouse to scramble out of her mouth, whole. Perhaps because I know the mice will keep coming.

My daughter caught cold the night we were evacuated. Her cough sounds like cotton ripping. I draw her into me, her spine between my breasts, the soles of her feet burning against my thigh. I curl around her like a shell around a soft snail. Even her fingers are hot, as if the fire entered her hand through the little burn. When I was a child I used to get in bed with my sister because I wanted to protect her from the devil. I believed the devil could draw her away through her dream, to a parallel universe, where there was a parallel city. Anything could be drawn out of this world, sucked into that one. Three years younger, she slept on her stomach. I'd put my nose in her hair. It had the colour and smell of unripe corn. She dreamed so strenuously that her cheeks were red, her lips slightly parted. I would lie on top of her, matching limb for limb. My arm over her arm, my leg over her leg. My fingers locked into hers. The way you lie flat if someone has fallen through the ice. The devil couldn't pull us both down. I'd hook the bone of her ankle between my toes. I could stop her from falling too deeply that way, by hooking the bone of her ankle, but that always woke her up and she'd throw me off her.

We went to see the Japanese performance artist. Wine glasses set in a circle like the numbers of a clock. Each wine glass filled with a different coloured spice. Grey-green, mustard, turmeric. He tipped the contents out on the floor and they floated down in gaseous clouds. On the video screen it looked like an aerial view of the earth. The way the earth looks like it's made of water and cloud, with nothing holding it together. The video cameras were as fragile as cheap toys. He attached wires to himself, a gas mask with a paper bag on the end, that filled and crumpled with his breathing. The screens showed a mushroom cloud exploding over and over, silently. Then he made a pyramid of the wine glasses and poured a jug of honey into them. The honey clung to the stems of the glasses until each glass was filled. It glistened in the spotlight, the whole pyramid one viscous city of glass. Then he put a syringe into his arm and poured his own blood into the glass, mixing it with his finger.

I was never interested in real estate before I met my mother-in-law. My husband's whole family punctuates every emotional event by buying or selling a house. It has taken me five years to recognize this pattern. Who would expect symbolism in Real Estate. But when I think of it, Louise has made it her life. There's her religion—a private part of her I can just barely guess the workings of—the fierce and protective love she has for her family, and Real Estate. I see all these parts of her bleeding into each other. The houses she has bought and sold are spread out over the city like clues in a scavenger hunt. Some houses she's sold three and four times to different families, noting the changes in wallpaper, carpet, light fixtures, as if the house has a camouflage that matches the families that move in. She will often point out houses that have ghosts. A house where a son murdered his mother of 73, and she was found two weeks later. Louise says this house is eternally on the market, like a lost soul that can't find bodies to move into it. She's bought houses for all her children, and when any of them tell a story they always start, When we were on Martin Street, or Suez Street, or Prince of Wales Street.

There's a small island of trees and grass near my house. My daughter and I played there tonight, to bring down the fever. It had snowed the night before, covering the bone-dry sidewalks, and another squall blew over in the afternoon. It was past Sarah's bedtime and my toes were cold in my rubber boots but we stayed out as long as we could. The streetlights threw perfect shadows from the trunks of the trees, thick straight columns like the Parthenon. An image drawn with sonar radar of a three-dimensional palace. I thought of Albert Austin and his Haiku books, of Philip's daughter playing in the snow of another continent. We trampled the snow but the columns still looked clean, the shadow edges hard.

I imagine a map of the city with plastic inlays of Louise's sales, family migration patterns from one neighbourhood to another. Each move changing their lives irrevocably and Louise is responsible for it. You sell a house to a customer, five years later they'll be back to you for another. There are only three things to think about in selling Real Estate. Location, Location, Location.

In India several years ago I was on a tour of a city palace. A guide separated me from the crowd, ushered me into a stone tower. Before I knew what was happening he had bolted the door and windows. No light leaked in. The darkness seemed to affect my inner ear and I swayed. Before I said anything he struck a match. There were thousands of convex mirrors imbedded in the walls. The guide, myself and the flame— reflected, wobbling. Our images splintered infinitely. Smashed but contained whole in each of the convex mirrors. The guide said, the Bridal Chambers, night of a thousand stars.

Purgatory's Wild Kingdom

Julian is thinking about a woman in Newfoundland. He's remembering Olivia preparing him a sardine sandwich, the way she laid each sardine on a paper towel and pressed the extra oil out of it. Then she cut off the head and tail, each sardine, until they were laid out carefully on the bread. Her head was bent over the cutting-board, her blond hair slid from behind her ear. He could see the sun sawing on her gold necklace. The chain stuck on her skin in a twisty path that made him realize how hot it was in the apartment. She was wearing a flannel pyjama top and nothing else, a coffee-coloured birthmark on her thigh. Eight years ago.

He's sitting at the kitchen table with a pot of coffee. His bare feet are drawn up on the chair, his knees pressed into the edge of the table. It's a wooden table-top that has been rubbed with linseed oil. There are scars from the burning cigarettes his wife occasionally leaves lying around. Small black ovals. There are thousands of knife cuts that cross over each other like the lines on a palm. He runs his finger over the table, tracing the grain of the wood. He pours another cup of coffee, and glances at the phone. Sometimes the university calls for Marika before ten, although they have been told not to do it. Marika requires only seven hours sleep, but if she's disturbed she's tired all day. She wakes up exactly at ten every morning. She's proud of the precision of her inner clock. Julian likes to pick up the phone before it rings twice. Lately the phone has been ringing and when Julian answers, nobody speaks.

Marika is fifteen years older than Julian. The people on this street are very rich. The brick houses are massive. Some of them have been broken into apartments and rented. There's almost no traffic. The trees block most of the noise. He and Marika don't know their neighbours. Once, while out taking photographs, Julian met a man three houses up who was

99

riding a sparkling black bike in circles. The man said he was Joe Murphy, of Joe Murphy's Chips, and they sold a large percentage of their chips in Newfoundland. He gave the silver bicycle bell two sharp rings.

"The bike's a birthday present from my wife. It's a real beauty isn't it?"

The tree shivered suddenly with wind and sloshed the bike with rippling shadows. Joe Murphy was wearing a suit and tie. The balls of his feet pressed against the pavement and there were sharp little crevices in his shined leather shoes. Julian noticed a crow leave a tree and fly straight down the centre of the street. He lifted his camera and took a picture of Joe Murphy. In the far distant corner of the frame is the crow. Julian leaves Joy Murphy out of focus, a blur in the centre of the picture, his face full of slack features. The crow is sharp and black.

"That makes me very uncomfortable," said Joe Murphy. "I think you have a nerve." He gave the bell another sharp ring, and pushed off the curb. His suit-jacket flapped on either side of him.

For the past two years Julian has been sleeping a lot. It's taken him two years to fall away from any kind of sleeping pattern. This way he's always awake at different hours. This seems exotic to him, but the cost is that he can't will himself to sleep. He sleeps in the afternoon and then finds himself awake at four in the morning. At dawn he's sometimes wandering around the neighbourhood. The light at dawn allows him to see straight into the front windows of the massive houses on their street, all the way to the back windows and into the backyards. It makes the houses seem like skeletons, with nothing hanging on the bones.

Sometimes Julian is asleep when Marika gets home from work. If there's no supper cooked for her she'll eat white bread and butter with spoonfuls of granulated sugar. Julian likes to cook for her and she likes what he cooks. But she's also happy to eat bread and sugar. She makes coffee and folds the bread and sinks it into her coffee. The soaked bread topples and she catches it in her mouth. The cats slink in from all the different rooms of the apartment and curl around her feet, or on her lap. She lifts the kitten and puts it inside her jacket. If Julian stumbles down the stairs, half awake, and he sees Marika bathed in the light of a baseball game on TV with her sugar bread, he feels that he has failed her. The sense of failure makes him even sleepier. He can't keep his eyes open.

Marika is not one for dwelling on the past. Julian knows very little about her past. Not that she's secretive. It's the kind of conversation that bores her. Marika has a powerful charm. She's a physics professor, but most of her friends are artists or writers. At parties, for conversation, she offers crystallized stories about nature or the stars. If someone interrupts her to ask about her parents, or something back in France, you can see the charm moving out of her face like a receding blush. She answers in only one or two sentences, faltering.

She thinks of memory only as a muscle that must be exercised to keep the whole mind sharp. She is interested in sharpness. If asked, she could recall exactly what she did on any date two years ago, she will remember what she wore, what Julian wore, what they ate, the content of any conversation that occurred on that day. But this is just a game.

Marika thinks about infinite tracts of time, about meteorogy, about hummingbirds, about measuring the erosion of coastlines, and whether the continents could still lock together like a jigsaw puzzle, or a jaw grinding in sleep. She thinks about fish that swim up the walls of fjords as if the walls were the lake bottom, or the tower of Babel. What such swimming against the stream does to their skeletons. When she isn't thinking things like this, she watches baseball, or drives in her car, or cooks, or she and Julian make love.

Julian has watched Marika simulate theoretical galaxies on the computer. She has found this program mostly to amuse him. He has seen two galaxies blinking together, dragging their sluggish amorphous bodies toward each other across the black screen. Each blink represents a million years, until they pass through each other. The gravitational pull of each galaxy affects the shape of the other until some stars are clotted in the centre, and the rest spread on either side of the screen like giant butterfly wings. Marika has shown him thousands of things like this. She has described the path of the plague in the middle ages, drawing a map on a paper napkin at Tim Horton's. She told him that in Egypt they have found the preserved body of a louse, on the comb of Nephretitti. A drop of human blood, perhaps Nephretitti's blood, was contained in the abdomen of the louse. They have discovered many things about ancient disease from that one drop of blood.

Julian collects every story Marika tells him. They often lose their scientific edges. He can't remember how old the louse was. For some reason the only thing he remembers about the plague is a costume. It was a long robe with the head of a bird. The doctor looked out through two holes cut in the feathered hood, over a protruding beak.

When he is awake Julian also pursues the moral of these stories. He keeps thinking they mean something other than what lies on the surface. Just as he can't imagine how much time it took to create the universe from a black hole, he can't get at that hidden meaning. The stories keep him in a state of awe.

Recently Marika contracted a virus, a nervous disorder. If not diagnosed, this disease can spread quickly through the body and destroy the tips of all nerve endings irreparably. It started with a numbness in Marika's left cheek. She had it checked immediately. Of course she had access to the best medical care in Toronto. The disease was arrested before any serious damage was done but the nerves in Marika's saliva ducts grew back connected to her tear duct. Now when she eats her left eye waters.

Julian has begun to suspect Marika. He wonders if she doesn't talk about her past because she is afraid she will seem like an old woman. It was the eye that fills of its own accord that started him thinking this way. The eye is the first sign of Marika's age. When her eye waters he's filled with fright. That fright causes its own involuntary reponse in him. He's remembering his past. Things he hasn't thought about in years. He has noticed that the skin on Marika's face looks older than before. The pores are larger. There are more wrinkles. The soft white pouches beneath her eyes are larger. That skin seems as vulnerable to him as the flesh of a pear he is about to bite.

He was going through their wedding photographs. He took them himself, so most of the pictures are of Marika. She is wearing a white kimono, and the apartment is full of white blossoms. Her face looks so much younger that for a moment he has the feeling the photographs have been doctored.

They're eating a dinner of lamb and fresh mint. Marika's knife is whining back and forth on the dinner-plate.

"Could you stop that noise?"

Marika's body jerks as if he has startled her, as if she didn't realize he was sitting beside her. "I was just lost in thought. I was thinking of a specimen of crab."

A tear is running down her cheek.

"In Guatemala," she says, "there's a species of crab that burrows into the ground and brings up in its claws shards of ancient pottery."

She lays down her knife and wipes a tear off her cheek with the back of her hand.

"The crabs descend beneath layer after layer to different cities that have been piled on top of each other, over time. Each city hundreds of years younger than the one below it. The crabs mix all the pottery shards together. All these ancient layers mixed together in the light of day. You really know very little about me. You know nothing about science."

Julian notices that both Marika's eyes are watering now.

In his dreams the stories Marika tells him are fables. He dreams about a crab that presents him with a jacket of glass shards that came from a wine bottle he once threw at Olivia. Olivia wears a cloak of stars, she opens her arms and the cloak is wrenched away from her, leaving her naked. She becomes two women, a blurred image, Marika and Olivia both.

Julian is walking past the ROM. The gargoyles outside are covered with burlap bags, like robbers with nylon stockings over their faces. A group of five people dressed in cartoon costumes emerge from a churchbasement into the glaring sun. They skip across the crosswalk, handing out flyers. Only the man in the Pink Panther costume trails behind. He has removed the head of the costume and carries it under his arm. The man's own head looks abnormally small against the giant pink neck of the costume. Julian takes a picture of him.

When Julian gets home he finds Marika asleep on the couch, a bowl of chips resting on her knee. She has fallen asleep in the middle of the afternoon with her wrist hanging over the rim of the chrome chip-bowl. The phone is ringing. Julian nearly trips over one of the cats in his rush to get it. Although it's ringing near Marika's ear, she doesn't stir. He picks it up but the person on the other end doesn't say anything. Julian hangs up and gently lifts Marika's wrist off the bowl. It takes him a long time to free the bowl but he does so without waking her.

This is a memory that Julian thinks about lately. The memory is lit with a big number one candle with monkey wrapped around it. Julian is carrying the cake. He can feel the yellow of the flame under his chin, like the shadow of a buttercup. He can see his daughter's face buried in Olivia's blouse, both their party hats sticking off the sides of their heads. There was a blizzard outside and Julian felt like they were wrapped in white tissue paper. He left a few days after that. He hasn't spoken to either of them since.

He's remembering things he hadn't noticed, even when they happened. He remembers a party in the country. Someone had shoved a hotdog wiener through a hole in a screendoor and every time the door slammed the hotdog wagged obscenely. It was the night he met Olivia. At midnight everyone went skinny dipping, the sound of diving bodies swallowed by the dark water. He was drunk and naked. When it came time to get out he suddenly felt embarrassed. He asked Olivia to give him a hand out of the water, so he could hold a towel in front of himself. When she did haul him out he managed to drop the towel and got caught in the skittering path of a flashlight.

Olivia's heels click down the hall through the loose pools of fluorescent light. It's Monday and the Topsail Cinemas mall is mostly deserted, except for the games arcade, which shoots out synchronized pings and buzzes. Most of the stores are undergoing various stages of renovation. The mall has looked this way all winter. Someone has been going at a cement wall with a jack-hammer. Chunks of cement have fallen away and rusted bars stick out. Everything is layered with powdered chalk and someone has drawn a skull and crossbones in the dust.

When Olivia turns the corner she sees the exhibit. A taxidermist from British Columbia named Harold. He's standing next to a chair, one hand on his hip, his index fingers looped through his change apron. When he sees Olivia he immediately becomes animated.

"Step this way beautiful, beautiful lady. Let me take you on a whirlwind tour of *Purgatory's Wild Kingdom*. Here you will see beasts miraculously wrested from the claws of decay. They have looked death in the eye. They have been consumed by death but they are not dust, thanks to the strange alchemy of embalming fluid and my own artistic wizardry, they live. They live."

He does this with a little flourish of his hands and a slight bow. Then he sighs as if he has used up all his energy. Pinching his nose with his thumb, he says, "$2.50 if you want to see it."

Olivia is twenty minutes early for the movie so she says, "Sure, I'll treat myself, why not, it's my birthday."

Harold has a thick mop of black hair with silver at the sides; his body is very tall and thin. One of his eyes is lazy, straying off to the side.

The display takes the shape of a mini-labyrinth made of ordinary office dividers. At each turn the viewer comes upon another stuffed animal.

"Most of them are from endangered species. But the truly unique thing about this exhibit is that these animals have all been hit by trucks. Trucks or cars. Every one of them. Please don't think I would ever hurt these animals for the sake of the collection. I collect them only after they have been killed.

"I'm different from those taxidermists you see on the side of the road during the summer, of course. I've seen them in this province, in Quebec and Alberta as well, lined up in the roadside flea markets next to tables that display dolls with skirts that sit over toilet-paper rolls. Those guys have a few birds maybe, a couple of squirrels mounted on sticks, a few mooseheads in the back of the station-wagon. I take my work more seriously than that. I am always trying to get a lively posture."

Olivia has stopped in front of a moose. The moose is making an ungainly leap over a convincingly weathered fence, one end of which had been neatly sawed off for the purposes of the exhibit. The moose is raised on its hind legs. Its head and neck are hunched into its shoulders, as if it were being repri-manded.

"This moose looks funny."

Harold pointed to the neck saying, "A less experienced man might have stretched the neck forward, and if I wished to be true to a moose in this position, that's what I would have done, but I don't work with the generic moose. I work with specific, individual moose. I took this artistic licence with the moose because it died on the hood of a station-wagon. The antenna of the car, unfortunately, entered its rectum and pierced the bowel twice, like a knitting needle. After that I felt this moose should be preserved in an attitude of shame."

"Are you serious?"

"I travel all over the continent with these animals, setting up in strip malls over the United States and Canada. I have a licence. It's educational. Ottawa pays me. I am very serious. People have to know what we are doing to our wild kingdom. I try to respect the animals as individual creatures. Every sentient being deserves a little respect. These animals, some of them, may never roam on the earth again. I keep them alive. Well I mean, they're dead, of course. But I have preserved them. My part is small, I guess. I'm like a red traffic light. That's how I see myself. I do my thing, I make them pause for a minute, before they march off into extinction. It's a chance to say goodbye. We can't forget what we've destroyed."

The last item is a polar bear. The office dividers are set up so that you come upon it suddenly. Its head and forepaws tower over the divider, but Olivia has been looking at a stuffed mother skunk and suckling skunks on the floor. When she walks around the corner she almost bangs into the bear. It makes her squeal as if she has suddenly slipped on ice. The animal's coat is yellowed, its jaw wide.

"She scared you," chuckles Harold and he pats the bear's coat twice, as if it's the bear that needs reassurance.

"This polar bear is my drawing card. The only animal not hit by a truck. This bear was shot. It wandered into a small town here in Newfoundland. It had been trapped on an ice flow. Starved. Dangerous. A mother bear separated from her cub. At seven in the morning a woman was putting out her garbage. It chased her back into the house. There was only an aluminum screen door between them. She got her husband's shotgun and when the bear crumpled the aluminum door, just like a chip bag, she shot it in the throat."

Harold parts the fur of the bear's throat. He has to stand on tippy toes to do so. Olivia can see the black sizzled hole, the fur singed pink.

At the end of the hall Olivia can see the woman in the ticket booth for the movie theatres. There's just one woman on tonight although the twin booth is also lit with flashing lights that circle the outline of the booths. The ticket woman has taken a Q-tip from her purse and is cleaning her ear.

"You have a truck outside?"

"Yes, an eighteen-wheeler."

"Would you consider joining me for a beer? I can give you my address and you can pick me up later. I have a daughter but I have a babysitter lined up for the evening. I was going out anyway."

Olivia has asked the taxidermist out for a beer because she suddenly feels sad about being alone on her birthday. She has an image of this man driving across an empty Saskatchewan highway with these wild beasts frozen in attitudes of attack, stretched in frozen gallops. He is the first person she has met in months who seems lonelier than she is. There is the chance he won't show up.

At the bar Olivia gets drunk very fast. Harold drinks the same bottle of beer most of the evening. At last call he buys himself another. He feels jumpy, excited. He's been on the road for six months now and almost always finds himself eating in empty hotel restaurants where the waitress watches a mini TV with an earphone so as not to disturb him.

Olivia is beautiful, Harold thinks. She's wearing a man's shirt, a moss-coloured material and grey leggings. When she walks to the bar he can see all the muscles in her long legs. She reminds him of a giraffe. Graceful despite her drunkenness and the fact that her legs are too long for her. Harold is adept at recognizing different kinds of drunkenness. In some people it twists free something bitter, but Olivia is blossoming. Her cheeks are flushed, Her Ss are lisping against her large front teeth. She has been telling him about the father of her child.

"It's like those animals in the back of your truck. All my memories. I can take them out and set them all over the bedroom and look at them, walk around them, all but touch them. Today is my birthday. I'm 30. But it feels like time hasn't moved at all since he left. I don't look any older. I'm just waiting, that's all. Do you know what I think? I think he'll be back. I know he will. I know how to get in touch with him if there's an emergency with Mary, my daughter. I've got the number in my bedside table. But I haven't called him since he left. I'm waiting until he comes to his senses. You know what I think? I think he's been enchanted by an ice queen. You know, a splinter of glass in his eye, but one of these days an unexpected tear is going to get it out. He'll be back, don't you worry, Harold."

Suddenly Harold is seized with worry. He removes his glasses. He puts his hand over hers on the table.

"Be honest with me now. Does it bother you that I have a wandering eye?"

Olivia lays down her beer glass and draws one knee up to her chest.

"At first it was strange, I didn't know which eye to look into."

"In some cultures it is thought to be auspicious. In some cultures it is a sign. I would like very much to go home with you this evening."

Olivia looks into his eyes, first one, then the other. Without his glasses they looked even stranger. They are flecked with gold, the lashes long and black like a girl's.

They are lying side by side in bed. Harold is already asleep, his cheek nuzzles into her armpit, her arm over her head. He had insisted on bringing the polar bear into the bedroom. He said it was his drawing card and that it was worth thousands of dollars. He couldn't afford to leave it in the truck. A gang of men in a Montreal parking-lot had broken into the truck, which was empty at the time, but he hadn't yet gotten the lock replaced.

The steps to Olivia's apartment were coated with ice and when they had gotten to the top, both of them sweating and straining with the bear, it had slipped and its head had thunked down the fifteen steps denting its cheek. This almost made Harold cry with frustration.

He said, "What an indecency for that poor creature, the most noble creature in the wild kingdom."

The thumping woke the babysitter who had fallen asleep on the couch. She pulled on her coat and boots and helped them with the polar bear although she was still half asleep. The second time they were successful.

The cold has sobered Olivia considerably. They end up lying in bed talking, with all their clothes on except for their shoes.

She says, "Harold, do you mind if we don't make love?" and he says, "Not at all," but he is very disappointed.

She talks more about the father of her child. She has a galaxy of glow-in-the-dark stars pasted onto the ceiling and when Harold removes his glasses the images are blurred and it looks as if they are really sleeping under the stars. While she talks he puts his hand under her shirt onto her belly. The warmth of it, and the small movement as she breathes is so charged with unexpected pleasure that Harold becomes almost tearful. He feels he can't trust his voice to speak, so he lies beside her silently. They both fall asleep.

Olivia's eight-year-old daughter, Mary, is awake in her bed, terrified. She has heard the thumping of something large and dangerous on the stairs outside, and drunken laughter and shouts. She hears whispers from her mother's room. She makes herself small against the headboard of the bed. She sits there watching the door of her room, waiting for something terrible to bash it open. She watches the clock radio with the red digital numerals change, change, change. Then she gets out of bed. She creeps along the wall to her mother's room. The hall light is on. She squeezes the brass doorknob with her sweaty hand and slowly, so the hinges won't creak, she pushes the door open. The light falls on the raging polar bear, frozen in the act of attacking her sleeping mother. Mary doesn't move. The bear doesn't move. Everything stays as it is for a long time until a man next to her mother raises himself up on his elbow and says, "Little girl?"

Mary slams the door and runs to the phone. She dials the number and it rings several times. She can hear her mother calling her. Then her father answers the phone. She says "Daddy, is that you?"

Julian has been awake, although it is four in the morning. He has been sitting on the couch holding Marika's hand. He hasn't moved her or disturbed her in any way since he took the chip-bowl from her, except to hold her hand. He says, "Yes, this is daddy."

He has been awake but it feels as if the child's voice has awoken him. He knew who she was but for a moment her name slipped his mind. For a moment, he could not for the life of him remember it.